I0590032

Not Always Lost

Not Always Lost

Tegan Morris

Magpie Publishing

© Copyright 2016 Tegan Morris

All rights reserved.

Tegan Morris asserts her moral right to be identified as the author of this work.

All rights reserved. No part of this publication may be produced or transmitted in any form or by any means, electronic or mechanical, including photocopying, recording or information storage and retrieval systems, without permission in writing from the copyright holder.

Email: teganmmorris35@gmail.com

Published by Magpie Publishing

This is a work of fiction. Names, characters, places, and incidents either are the product of the author's imagination or are used fictitiously, and any resemblance to actual persons, living or dead, events, or locales is entirely coincidental.

A catalogue record for this book is available from the National Library of New Zealand.

Prologue

Sitting at the side of the stage and looking out into the crowd was like looking down from a great height. "What am I doing here? I'm not prepared for this!" Shannon thought to herself. Her guts were twisting in knots, and she couldn't remember how to breathe. The principal was still talking. The last part of her speech was sounding more and more like the final countdown before the skydivers hurl themselves out into space. Looking out into the crowd of blurring faces, Shannon spotted Katey's reassuring smile. As they held eye contact Shannon saw Katey tap her chest, followed by an in and out gesture. That was something to focus on. "In," Shannon chanted silently to herself, drawing in a deep slow breath. "Out," she exhaled fully. She still felt charged with nerves and expectation, but she felt slightly less panicky.

Now the principal was announcing Shannon as the next speaker, jolting her out of the calming bubble created by her focused breathing. It was time to face the music.

There was polite applause, as Shannon moved to centre stage. Closing her eyes for a heartbeat, she took one final long breath. Koro Artie's words echoed in her head:

"...believe it and you'll do it, girl." Shannon opened her eyes and focused back on the audience. This was her moment. With strengthened resolve, she began to speak.

Chapter One

Thinking about the evening she was going to be spending with Richard, Shannon opened the car door and climbed in. Pitching her armload of shopping bags onto the passenger seat, she sent off a text message, "On my way-xox".

Putting the car into gear, she pulled out onto the busy road and accelerated into the traffic. Smiling and humming along to the radio, she began to mentally list off all the things she needed to do. Being head of the student council was a big responsibility — it involved people managing and diplomacy with both students and teachers. It also meant organizing meetings, writing reports, keeping notes and maintaining her academic performance — not to mention her social life.

Life was pretty good, Shannon thought. There had been a few bad decisions and things that she regretted, but really, what teenager hadn't made at least one mistake or had something to regret? Though, for Shannon her mistakes had been more serious than most. Two and a half years ago Shannon and her mum had packed up their lives and started over in a new town. The hasty relocation to a new community and a new school had been to avoid the drama and fallout of the "situation".

It wasn't something Shannon would ever look back on lightly, but even at this point in her life she could see that things could have turned out much worse than they did. In fact, right now, it made everything she had these days seem that much sweeter.

This time round she had found Richard, a caring, sweet and intelligent boyfriend, who seemed determined to stick with her. They had been dating for the last year and a half, and they had become very close. Richard was one person in Shannon's life who she had really opened up to. She felt there were no secrets between them. Shannon was also making a big effort at school, where she worked hard to build a good reputation with her classmates and teachers. It was all part of Shannon's bigger picture, which she had mapped out carefully. She was aiming to finish high school on a positive note, with everything in order. There was no way she was going to risk messing up her future, after already getting a second chance.

Seeing her phone flash at the corner of her vision, Shannon swiped the screen by reflex. Still preoccupied with her thoughts, she chanced a look down to the screen. A message from Richard flashed up. "Cant wait to show you my new skills. See you soon sweet thing!" Shannon smiled at his cheesy lines — she loved his sense of humour and charm. She started to tap out a reply. She heard screeching brakes — and then everything turned to chaos. Sounds of ripping metal and shattering glass filled the air. It felt like a giant had punched the side of the car and then shaken it for good measure. Suddenly the madness stopped. Shannon found herself slumped in the driver's seat.

She couldn't see clearly. Everything was blurred down to a small patch directly in her line of sight. It was like looking through a snowstorm. A blur which became a police officer was running towards her. Leaning in through the shattered window, he was saying something, but Shannon couldn't make out the words over the ringing in her ears and the all-encompassing numbness. The police officer kept talking to her, and she was trying to pay attention. She wanted to answer him but all her muscles had frozen. She tried to respond by blinking, but each time her eyes closed it was harder to open them again. Everything faded to nothing as her mind escaped to a black emptiness.

Chapter Two

Drifting on a rising tide of consciousness, emerging from the dark, Shannon found herself in a hazy white space. Gradually the blurry confusion began to resolve. She was lying on a flat bed. As she looked around, the tiled ceiling and white drapes enclosing her swam into greater clarity. Lying still, she tried hard to focus her senses, noticing the steady mechanical beeps and muffled sounds of voices nearby. She wondered how much time had passed. Had she been unconscious for hours or days?

With the regaining of awareness came an avalanche of pain. It was a struggle to maintain focus and to not just fall back into the darkness. Just as Shannon was about to drop back into nothingness, she heard her mother's frantic voice somewhere nearby. She couldn't pick out words, but she could hear the rise and fall of her mother's increasingly agitated voice and the measured response of someone else. Shannon wanted to reassure her mum. Using the awareness of pain as an anchor, she tried to call out. Her voice barely came out in a squeak. "Urggh."

Trying to be calm, Shannon focused back on her body, mentally cataloguing the different sensations and trying to get movement. "Everything hurts," was her overwhelming impression, as the various sensations started to fully register. Dull aches deep in her bones, pulsating spasms of tormented nerves, and throbbing sensations of varied intensity radiated through her system. Pinpointing whether there was a beginning or ending to each seemed impossible. The worst pain radiated from her head, the rest spattering down her torso and stopping at her waist. It was a relief to find one part of her body that wasn't incredibly painful.

Shannon spent some time struggling to make her arms respond. After a while, moving her awareness down her body, she started wondering, "Why aren't my legs feeling like the rest of me?" Painfully she inched her hand down so it was resting on her thigh. When her hand finally lay where her leg should be, Shannon realized that there was no response. She could feel her fingers, but it was like they were touching a piece of pliant wood. Her fingers told her it was warm and yielding as her leg should be, but there was no response from her leg when her fingers pressed down. She should be able to feel the touch, no matter how light. The warmth of her palm should be obvious. Beginning to panic, Shannon groaned in pain as she turned her head slightly within the confines of the stiff brace, to see her hand really was resting on her mid-thigh. Five words rasped from her mouth.

"I... I can't feel my legs!"

Panic gripped her and the breath caught in her throat. Within seconds, a cacophony of piercing alarms filled the room. A nurse appeared at her side.

"Richard... help me... what, Mum?" Shannon gasped in a ragged chant of panic and confusion. The nurse replied in a soothing voice.

"It's okay Shannon... listen dear... take some deep breaths."

But Shannon's mind was too frantic and beyond reason, overwhelmed by fear and desperation. When the nurse's attempts to calm Shannon didn't work, she took out a syringe of fluid which she swiftly injected into the IV line. A stinging sensation and a chill spread up Shannon's arm and throughout her body as the sedative took hold.

"... my legs..." were the last words that passed Shannon's lips, before everything faded out again.

Chapter Three

Scratching his unshaven jaw in a distracted way, Richard reread the latest message as he walked into Advanced Geometry. The text had come in last night from Shannon's mum.

"Shay woke up but things got a bit overwhelming so they gave her something to sleep... now running extra tests. Doing well though – Evelyn."

Tension rippled through his shoulders and the knot tightened in his gut, as he stared at the characters on the screen. The unsettled and stressed feeling had sat with him since he first heard about Shannon's accident, had increased every day that there was no positive news.

His scowl deepened as the words "overwhelming" and "extra tests" banged about in his head. Sighing, he tried to ease his tense muscles, struggling to keep his emotions under control.

The last five days had taken their toll on Richard. Numerous feelings had been continuously swirling in his head, denial and worry being top of the list. With no idea how to deal with them, he shoved them to the back of his mind in an effort to keep himself together.

Distracted by this ongoing internal battle, Richard walked past his usual seat and took an empty spot near the back of the class. As he stared down at the phone on his knee, the clamour of the class became a background hum.

Since he had first got the call from Shannon's mum he had spent his time in a state of shock.

"...Shannon... in hospital... huge crash!"

He became aware that the words, which were replaying in his mind, were now being echoed around him. This brought his attention back to his surroundings. The girls in front of him were leaning across the aisle, whispering in shocked tones about Shannon.

Rich briefly met the eyes of one of the two girls as they glanced at him. Slouching in his seat, he clenched his jaw in frustration. It seemed like the school gossip mill was having a field day. He reached into his pocket and cranked up the volume on his music player, intending to block everything out.

Rich was trying to avoid as many people as possible, taking different routes to classes and entering and leaving class as close to the bell as possible. Despite this preoccupation, or because of it, time was crawling by. His efforts to avoid his classmates were disrupted by text messages.

"What's happening dude, is Shannon ok? Haven't seen her round~ Steve"

"Send our love to Shay when you see her~ Bex"

"I can't believe what's happened with Shannon, let me know if we can help somehow~Rachael"

Each message added to Richard's mental turmoil. "I just need a break from this. I don't have anything to tell people. I wish they'd just cut me some slack," Rich thought to himself, weighing the phone in his hand. When it buzzed again a minute later, that was the last straw. Jabbing the power off button, he tossed it angrily into his bag.

Over the next couple of days of school, Rich kept holding together his front of composed isolation. "Keep your head down," he told himself. "Don't let them see what you're feeling. It will just make it worse." It was getting harder to pretend he wasn't noticing the increasing number of suspicious looks from his peers. Their reaction made him think they hadn't forgotten his troubled past. Groups of students would stop talking as he walked past. Others would shoot nervous glances at him, as if they expected him to explode. Ignoring the unwanted attention, he carried on. But by lunch time of the third day after hearing that Shannon had woken up, Richard's resolve was wearing thin.

The thought of the unchecked messages choking his inbox was adding to his anxiety. Making his way through the lunchtime crowd, he dug around in the bottom of his bag and hesitantly pulled out his phone. His conscience had been prodding him. "What if you get another update? What if something's happened?"

He had thirty-two unchecked messages, a glaring reminder of his neglect. With a sinking feeling in his stomach, he scrolled down. At least seven were from Shannon, a couple from her mum, including a voice message, and the rest from his friends. As he flicked through the texts, the messages from Shannon seemed like they were spelled out in neon on the screen.

"I miss you! xx~Shay"

"I'm scared. I need to see you....please. xx~ Shay"

"I hope you're okay~Shay"

"Why aren't you replying?~Shay"

"I love you~ Shay"

Rich felt the frustration start to simmer under his skin. Everyone was focused toward Shannon. But no one had thought to check on him. It brought back memories and feelings from years before — but that was just another thing he didn't want to think about right now.

He violently tossed the phone into his bag and joined the lunch line at the cafeteria, keeping his head down as he tried to deal with his feelings about the messages. Those few words from Shannon had started his head spinning again. He couldn't decide whether to be more relieved or more anxious, now that she had made contact. There was both the impulse to respond immediately and to continue to ignore the situation. A vortex of confused feelings and conflicting thoughts threatened to overwhelm him.

Standing in the line, he overheard voices talking about Shannon yet again. For the last few days she had been the main topic of discussion at school. There had been a lot of speculation and gossip over the details, and Rich couldn't face challenging any of it. Keeping his head low, he heard an annoying nasal voice, questioning someone about what they knew. He recognized the answering voice as one of his friends, replying with a non-committal, "Dunno".

"Seems like there's a lot of rumours about what happened. What do you reckon about the story that she was drunk after partying with the rugby team...?" the voice persisted. "...And can you give me a comment about Rich's reaction to the allegation that she was sexting him when she crashed... ?"

Rich knew he was about to explode. He elbowed his way through the line, ignoring disgruntled muttering. He grabbed the guy by the shoulder and spun him around.

"Quit talking crap about me. You don't know anything about what's going on!" he continued, recognizing the individual as a member of the school magazine club. "Same goes for everyone else," he barked, glaring at the curious faces around him. "But you," he continued, jabbing a finger at the nosey dickhead in front of him, "can tell all the other gossip-mongering parasites to mind their own business!"

He turned and made to leave, his fists clenched tightly at his sides, lunch forgotten.

The same annoying voice called after him: "Seems like someone's got a guilty conscience."

Before he could stop himself, Richard swung back around, with his arm drawn back ready to punch the smart-mouthed twerp. Suddenly, he felt a strong grip on his elbow.

"Hold up there, Mike Tyson. This is not the boxing ring!" cut in the firm voice of the deputy principal.

"Everybody else, get back to your lunch!" she bellowed to the small crowd that had assembled.

"Come with me, sonny Jim." Ms Maclean said, as she turned and strode out the door.

As he closed the door to the deputy principal's office, Richard steeled himself for a stern lecture.

"Mr Martens, I am concerned at this sudden return to your previous misconduct. Violence is unacceptable in this school." Richard took a breath, about to answer. She held up her hand to stop his response.

"But, I understand with recent events that you have been under some extra strain." At these words, Richard felt a tremor run through his body. "It's important that you, as much as Shannon and her family, know that there are people who care. Which is why, I want you to know that if I can be of support please feel free to come and speak to me." These words sank into Rich's mind. It was such a relief to have someone acknowledge his feelings.

Later, as he stood outside the administration building, feeling shattered and trying to gather his thoughts, his friend Jason approached him. "Hey man, I hope Ms Maclean wasn't too harsh on you. I totally would have smacked that jerk at lunch if he'd said that to me."

"Yeah, she was okay about it. She let me off pretty light, with everything going on with Shay." At the thought of her, Rich felt his stomach drop. It was like his insides were some blank rattling space, left empty by the absence of direction and confidence that normally resided there. Receiving praise, having Shannon on his arm, and the resulting positive attention had for a long time given Richard a sense of stability and control.

"Speaking of Shay, do you have plans to go see her soon? I know my girlfriend would be pissed if I didn't visit when she was sick." Jason spoke up again.

"Umm, yeah?" Rich replied uncertainly. "I just hadn't figured out the right time." He could normally keep everything in perspective. But now the things that boosted him up and helped him feel successful and in control were gone. All this accident stuff with Shannon had ripped it away. He needed that security, the respect and the admiration back. Shannon was the key to this, he realized. Every aspect of his place within the social network of the school had her involvement. Before Shannon, he had been a social outcast that everyone avoided because he'd gotten into a few fights.

"What if things are really serious? ... What can I do? ... No. Everything will be fine. I'm sure the doctors will help her." Richard's thoughts continued to swing back and forth, between positivity and doubt. Part of him still wanted to run far away from the situation, but the other part held out hope that reconnecting with his girlfriend would get him back on track. With this new clarity and plan of action, Rich got through the rest of his classes feeling better than he had in days.

Chapter Four

Having found a parking space near the hospital, Richard killed the engine and stared blankly through the windscreen. Anxiety and anticipation pressed in on him. Fear and doubt encircled him like a net, trapping him in his seat. Despite the new clarity, he still had an urge to run. The heavy silence was interrupted by his fingers' increasingly agitated staccato drumming on the steering wheel.

He told himself that finding out what was going on was crucial, so that he could make sense of what was happening. Things would get back to normal, he knew it; this was only a bump in the road before the rest of their lives.

Richard grabbed his phone and hit speed dial. He sighed in relief as Shannon answered in a cheerful, if slightly raspy voice. Enthusiasm and joy seeped through the phone, caressing and reassuring him. Rich soaked up the warmth in her voice. It was so good to hear her and to make that connection again. As they talked he was able to cast aside the doubt and fear.

Ending the call, he basked in a familiar and welcome sense of security which had seeped into the void of anxiety and overwhelming uncertainty. But that was quickly cut short when he remembered that he hadn't yet listened to the voicemail message left by Shannon's mum. Dialling, he listened impatiently to the static-filled recording. "We need to talk... something ... need to ... you ..." were the words he could make out. Disconnecting the call, Rich refused to let his mind run away with worry, but the doubts had already swept back in, drowning the small spark of comfort that had briefly rested in his centre.

Entering through the automatic doors of the hospital, Rich was blasted by a jet of warm air, carrying with it a scent of disinfectant and fried food. The smell both unsettled and grounded him in its unwanted familiarity. This moment of sensory shock was not the only thing that slowed Rich's steps right now. Worrying about Shannon's condition was dominating his thoughts. His state of mind over the past few days, and the hollow that had gaped open after the lunchtime fight, unnerved him enough to keep walking. At least this way he felt he was doing something to regain control of a situation that no one really seemed to understand.

When he reached the ward, Rich was just about to ask a frazzled looking nurse where he could find Shannon Carlisle's room, when he spotted her mum Evelyn, sitting alone in a row of cold clinical waiting room chairs. Evelyn's usually carefully polished appearance was gone. Her make-up was smudged and her clothes were creased. "Mrs Carlisle," he called hesitantly, barely audibly. He cleared his throat and tried again. "Evelyn."

She looked up. Stumbling to her feet, she enveloped him in a tight hug. Richard's arms rose to encircle her by reflex. For several minutes they stood together, until she stepped back and pulled him over to a seat.

"Richard, I'm so glad you're here. There's something I need

to tell you before you see Shay," she said, looking at him with an anxious drawn expression. "Shay is being monitored for an injury to her spine... At the moment they have said her legs don't have any voluntary movement or feeling. So they want to keep her back immobile till they can figure out how serious things are."

Rich felt everything around him zero down to the words coming out of Evelyn's mouth. They were crystal clear in his ears, but his brain just couldn't decipher the meaning.

He paused at the door to Shannon's room, steeling himself. Tapping twice on the door, he pushed it open slightly and poked his head into the dimly lit room. Blinking, he adjusted his vision and focused on the white covered bed in the centre of the room. Shannon was lying flat, with the sheets pulled up high. For a moment her stillness and the atmosphere of the room made his fear almost overwhelming.

"Hey, is that you Rich?" Shannon's voice rose from the bed.

Hearing her speak broke the spell that had held him frozen with his hand still on the door. "Hey, yeah, it's me," he answered, stepping closer to the bed.

Shannon was wearing a hospital gown, which made her normally tan skin look washed out and grey. With a half-smile, she beckoned him closer. For a second Richard hesitated, before stepping towards her. He cautiously leaned in to give her an awkward halfway hug. As he stepped back, he noticed the wires and tubes attached to his girlfriend's arms and disappearing under the covers. Around the room there were numerous machines making sounds and flashing numbers and symbols. It all felt very intimidating.

"I better not knock anything in here," Richard blurted, as he shuffled about the space, "I don't want to get yelled at again."

For a moment Shannon's face lit up at his clumsy

movements, which brought back memories of their first school dance, with his stiff awkward steps as they had moved together. "Do you want to sit?" she asked, lifting her hand to indicate the two chairs next to the bed.

Hesitating, Richard sat in the seat furthest from the bed. The chair felt uncomfortable, with its stiff vinyl covering and hard metal frame. Being surrounded by all that medical equipment didn't make him feel any more at ease.

Occupied with his own worries and insecurities, he didn't notice the look of hurt and disappointment that passed over Shannon's face.

So many feelings were bashing around in his head: worry, fear, anger. Evelyn's words rang in his ears, tormenting him. The whole situation seemed impossible. Only two weeks ago they had spent a carefree weekend, kicking up waves in the Coromandel, now her she was in a hospital bed.

Shannon's voice seeped into his thoughts and he realized that he had missed what she had said. Shaking his head, he tuned in to what she was saying.

"So, how much have I missed at school?" Shannon asked. "It's so hard to keep track of the time, let alone what day it is." She was trying to draw him into a normal conversation.

"Ugh, not much. Everything is pretty much the same..." Richard responded slowly. The silence was heavy between them. What did school matter, when she was in here, hooked up to all these machines, he thought?

The expectant pause continued to hang in the room, and Shannon could feel that there was something left unsaid.

Richard was shifting his weight in his seat. He uttered a small "What..."

Shannon looked at him expectantly, her gaze steady.

Clearing his throat, Richard tried to dislodge the words that were choking him.

"What happened, Shay? Do you remember what happened?"

Shannon sighed. She should have expected this. That was a question that had been asked too often lately, and it was one she still couldn't entirely answer.

She took a deep breath. "Rich, I honestly don't. I remember I was shopping for school, and that's it. And you. I was thinking of you. That's the last thing I remember."

Her words were a punch to Richard's gut. Guilt spread through him. He was texting her that afternoon.

His eyes roamed over the machines and equipment in the room again. It all seemed more harmless, the longer he looked at everything; he even began to vaguely recognize some of the machines. The jumping lines on the screen to the left of the bed reminded him that it was the heart-rate monitor, and the box-like machine attached to a tube going into Shannon's arm was an IV drip. "Probably for her pain meds," he thought to himself.

But when he brought his eyes back to Shannon, he couldn't help but let his gaze linger where her legs lay under the cover. It was hard to get his head round the idea that something that looked so normal was no longer a functioning part of the whole person that was his girlfriend.

Shannon continued to try to maintain a normal conversation. "How are the committee's plans for the end of season party going? ... I hope Rachael doesn't forget to confirm the DJ..."

Eventually she ran out of questions and the conversation died. As the silence stretched out, Richard became restless.

"... I probably should get going, need to get my assignment

done..." Rich stood up, pausing awkwardly in the middle of the room.

Shannon once again unsteadily raised her arms in expectation of a hug. "I missed you, Rich. I'm glad you came to see me." As she closed her arms around him, she turned her face to kiss him, as they usually would when parting. But he had turned his head away. Her familiar scent was replaced by the sterile, chemical smell of hospital.

He was just about to open the door to leave when he heard Shannon almost whisper, "I love you."

Pausing, he turned back and kissed her forehead. "See you later," he said over his shoulder, as he walked out the door.

Chapter Five

"I'm so glad you're coming home now, it's been lonely having the house to myself," Evelyn said cheerfully.

"Yeah, me too," Shannon responded noncommittally, her thoughts drifting back to the day she had left to go shopping and not come back.

Knowing that she wouldn't be going back to stay at the rehab unit was exciting. But the unknowns of returning home and facing reality gave her a sense of anxiety that bubbled in the pit of her stomach. Although she was grateful to have escaped without any significant injury to her senses or brain, it was still such an uphill battle. Shannon felt that the accident had punched open a huge gaping hole in her future. Everything she'd planned and worked for seemed impossible now – things like leaving home and attending university.

She'd felt safe and almost comfortable in the hospital and then the rehabilitation centre. The routines and almost cocoon-like atmosphere, along with the expertly trained staff, had made Shannon feel safe; so much so that false tendrils of hope started to sprout in her mind. They all knew just what to do and say, nobody looked strangely at the young woman in the chair. Being around people in various stages of ill health and recovery had provided a brief but misleading sense that things were okay, and that such injuries and illnesses were temporary.

On the weekend after her return home, Evelyn persuaded Shannon that a shopping trip would be good for them both. Shannon agreed. She enjoyed shopping, and was looking forward to a day out. She started the morning struggles of getting out of bed and preparing for the day with more enthusiasm than usual.

But right from the beginning, things started going wrong.

For a start, Shannon realised that she couldn't wear her favourite outfit. The beautiful dress, with a long and swishy skirt, was no longer a suitable part of her wardrobe, as she risked getting it tangled in her wheels. She felt frumpy wearing practical sweatpants and a hoodie.

Next, Shannon rolled into the bathroom to fix her hair and makeup. With frustration, she realized that she couldn't see the mirror from her wheelchair.

"Mum." Shannon called half-heartedly, "Mum...!" she called again, louder. "I can't believe I have to ask for help with this," she thought, as Evelyn appeared at the door.

"Can you help with my makeup, please? The main mirror is too high and this compact is really tiny and blurry. I don't even know if I've got my foundation on right."

"Uh, sure love." Evelyn reached for the eye pencil. "Your skin looks fine; just want me to do your eyes?"

Leaning forward, she paused, scrunching her forehead in concentration. "It's a bit different doing it for someone else," she said, tentatively applying the colour.

After several frustating minutes of Evelyn fussing with different makeup products, Shannon lost patience. "It's fine, mum," she said bluntly, as she peered into the compact mirror. "Thanks, but we should go before the lunchtime rush."

Then, they had problems getting a park at the mall. They had to circle the parking lot several times before finding a spot with space for Shannon to negotiate the transition from the car to her chair, while Evelyn hovered anxiously. Everything was still new and a struggle. Shannon felt self-conscious as she worked through the steps her occupational therapist had taught her. Approaching the entrance to the mall, she felt Evelyn take hold of the chair and begin to push her along. "I can do it myself, LET GO!" she snapped, as she propelled herself away from her mother and rode into the mall.

After a couple of hours of shopping, the tension had eased somewhat between mother and daughter, but they were still not saying much to each other. Shannon and Evelyn sat down to lunch in the food court. As they ate, Shannon contemplated her earlier outburst, and was considering a peace offering to her mum, when a stranger walked up to their table. Smiling brightly at them both, the woman addressed Evelyn: "How is the young lady doing today?"

Evelyn looked between her daughter and this strange woman with a surprised expression. "It's so nice that you bring your daughter out shopping, it must be so challenging. I truly admire people in your difficult situation. I honestly don't know how you manage." As the cheerful stranger said this, she reached out and pressed her hand to Evelyn's arm, in an earnest comforting manner. Shannon could feel the heat of frustration rising through her body, both at her mother for not telling this stranger where to get off and this woman for her obnoxious, condescending manner.

Turning to Shannon, the lady patted her cheek and said in the most sugary voice, "What a lovely face. Such a shame about your limitations, I'm sure you would have been a heartbreaker. Take care, sweetie," before turning and disappearing into the crowd.

For Shannon this was the final straw. "I'm out of here! See you at the car," she snapped. Grabbing the keys from the table, she began winding her way through the maze of tables to the exit.

On the drive home, Shannon sat numbly looking out the window, while Evelyn kept up a stream of cheerful conversation, seemingly unaware of Shannon's dark mood.

"Did you see that sparkly top in Glassons? It's your colour Shay, Rich would agree, I'm sure..."

"... Or how about that gorgeous frilly skirt I pointed out? It would look lovely with your black halter neck..."

"... I saw a display in the window at Bags & Things, Shay and you wouldn't believe it but just last week Vanessa had the same clutch purse at the exhibition opening. $750, so she said... but the price tag read $120!! Honestly, I don't know why some people exaggerate so much!"

This constant upbeat chatter had become Evelyn's standard tactic since Shannon had regained consciousness. If there wasn't someone speaking with purpose, and silence descended, it seemed impossible for Evelyn to remain quiet.

Evelyn was trying to keep a positive face and encourage her daughter. But she had never really known how to connect with Shannon, and this present situation made it much worse. It had been the same before Shannon's pregnancy, although they had become closer after her granddaughter Louise was born.

"(Sigh) Oh gosh, I forgot to mention that I read in the paper the other day that the council are planning on renovating the netball court clubhouse where you girls spend so much of your time! Won't that be nice Shay!"

Shannon stared angrily out of the window in silence.

When they arrived home, Shannon got herself out of the car as quickly as she could, snappily rejecting Evelyn's offers of help. She fled through the house, slamming the back door as she rolled down the new ramp into the back garden, picking up speed. Reaching ground level, her chair had so much momentum it sailed on and rammed into the back fence, jerking Shannon forwards in her seat. Tears of frustration welled up and came out as sobs as she rammed her chair repeatedly into the fence, taking some satisfaction from the jarring sensation.

As her tears gradually abated, she heard humming coming from the opposite side of the fence. It wasn't just humming, it was the sound of the old man who lived next door, moving about in his garden. The repetitive swish-scrape of his rake fell into rhythm with the thump of her chair against the fence. It was hard to stay wound up with the soothing sounds. Gradually as the intensity of feelings seeped away, Shannon was left with tears that hadn't yet run themselves dry. While she was still trying to settle the sobs that kept hiccupping out of her, she heard the old man addresing her.

"What's up, girly?" he said in a cheerful tone. "You're looking a bit low. Did someone let the air out of your tires?" he joked.

"Leave me alone, I'm having a bad day!" Shannon replied sulkily.

There was silence for a bit, interrupted by the old man softly singing something that sounded suspiciously like "Nobody likes me, everybody hates me, I'm going down the garden to eat worms," as he raked leaves, interspersed with the sound of Shannon's chair still thumping against the wooden boards.

Finally the old man looked over the fence at Shannon and spoke again. "If you don't want to tell me what's wrong, how about you tell me what your name is, ne kotiro," he said calmly.

Shannon looked up into his kind, sun-weathered face. His brown eyes seemed full of life.

"My name's Shannon, my friends call me Shay." she sniffled. There was a long pause. "Everything is so awful now...it's all so hard! I can't do anything like I used to... everything feels like it's falling a-a-part and I don't ev-ev-even know if I can put the pieces back to-g-g-gether."

Her neighbour answered as he approached a gap in the fence. "You might not believe me, but I know a thing or two about what it's like to lose something that seems so important."

"How could you know anything like what I'm going through?" Shannon sniffed.

"Look here," he said, leaning closer. Shannon noticed the shortened sleeve where most of his left arm was missing. "As tough as things might seem now, there can be a bright future for you. Just wait and see. That chair won't stop you from getting where you want to go."

Chapter Six

Shay was surprised at how quickly she became friends with her neighbour, from that first day when they'd exchanged names. For many years Shannon had avoided communicating with most adult males. She distrusted them all after her dad's vanishing act when she was fourteen. Over the days and weeks that followed, Shannon and Koro Artie often talked across the fence. She realized that he did actually understand some of what she was going through, unlike so many of the other well-meaning visitors and professionals. She could see he was living his life and seemed happy, despite his missing arm. Even with these realizations, it was a struggle to come to terms with what he had said to her on their first meeting.

"It's what you do with what's between your ears that counts. You can be just as great as you thought you would have been before. You might just have to work a bit harder or try a different path to get there."

Shannon finally began to see that there might still be a future for her to work towards. But it was such a huge unknown. It was scary. To begin thinking now, that the secure, hopeful future she had planned was no longer possible in her present condition, made Shannon cling even more stubbornly to the idea that she could and would get something of her old life back. It was too much to have to accept that life would be full of challenges that would have to be fought from a wheelchair. She put the thoughts of the future aside and focused on the prospect of recovery.

Determination and pride were Shannon's weapons against the anxiety that hovered as she faced the prospect of returning to high school. It had been two months since the last time she had entered the gates of her school. Those days seemed like they were from an entirely different lifetime, one where she had confidence, purpose and a strong sense of connection. Now she didn't know what sort of reaction she would be facing. It was like the first day of school all over again.

The parade of blank faces Shannon passed in the crowded halls was an unsettling start to her return. Many people didn't seem to know how to approach her. There was a sea of faces that in the past had always acknowledged her with a smile and a wave, or a call of "Hi Shay", often followed by some question about the one of the committees she was part of. Many of these same people now turned away or suddenly became blind and dumb in her presence. It was not altogether unexpected, but still hurtful. An awkward hush fell over a group of classmates as Shannon approached. Fixing a bright smile on her face, she greeted them. Immediately their eyes dropped to the floor, walls or ceilings as they muttered awkward greetings in return. It was a blow to her pride and steadily falling confidence.

Shannon promised herself that she would not let others see that she was hurt. At this moment, she heard herself being hailed from further down the hall. "Shannon! OMG, how have you been? We've missed you soooo much!" This exclamation was followed by the over-bright flashy grin of someone she only vaguely recognised.

"Jessie? Oh, yeah hi."

"Wow, what's the go with you?" Jessie's two shadows leant in closer, waiting for Shannon's reply.

"Not a lot, just getting back into school. Catching up with class. Standard stuff."

"Well you're looking stunning, really... healthy again, considering..." An insincere smile curled around Jessie's bottom lip momentarily, then vanished. Her two deputies' faces mirrored Jessie's expression. "See you around Shannon."

Shannon paused, unsure of what had just happened, as Jessie's approach was totally unexpected, given they'd never had cause to interact. As she struggled through the day, all this strange attention started to wear on Shannon's nerves.

Moving through the hallways, students mostly stepped around her or parted to let her through. Occasionally someone would scuff her shoulder with their bag, or she would have to swerve drastically to avoid someone walking into her. "Seriously!" she thought to herself in irritation as she dodged another person who had just about tripped over her, "I don't know how people aren't walking into walls all the time. Everyone is so busy with their phones or talking. It's like they don't even notice what's in front of them." Sighing, she gritted her teeth and made one final push to get to the student bathroom.

She had just shoved her way through the heavy door and into the main area of the bathroom by the sinks when one of her friends from the netball team came barging into the room. "Shay!" she greeted with a sincere smile, "It's so good to have you back!" she exclaimed, swooping over and wrapping Shannon in a sudden hug.

"It's good to see you too, but what was that for?" Shannon asked in confusion, as she was slowly released by her enthusiastic friend.

"It's been ages since we've seen each other, so I thought I would break the ice... Besides, you looked like you needed cheering up a bit," Katey replied, as she stepped back to give her friend some space. "There's so much we have to catch up on. I have to tell you about all the developments in the student committee and all the other news around school." She continued, leaning against one of the sinks: "How about I come over next weekend and we can catch up? I'll even bring a couple of good movies if you can provide the popcorn!"

Shannon considered Katey's proposal. It had been ages since she had really hung out with any of her girlfriends properly. But things were so different at home... All the clumsy and bulky equipment and ramps... but in the end, the desire for company and a fun movie marathon won over the caution. "Sure... I guess. Let's arrange something later" she replied with a smile.

Chapter Seven

Days passed, and Shannon saw very little of Richard. Every potential meeting had been thwarted by some excuse for his absence. It frustrated her, but being so focused on just moving from class to class took precedence over these thoughts. By the middle of her second week back, Shannon was building confidence in manoeuvring the chair, and she decided to go visit Richard out at the sports centre. Just as she was about to round the corner, she heard Richard talking in an agitated tone, something made her pause to listen. She knew eavesdropping wasn't a good idea, but what she heard made her come to an abrupt stop.

"Do you know what's annoying? When you have to bend down to kiss your girlfriend like she's a kid. People stare all the time, probably wondering what's wrong with her and why she's in a chair. I can't talk to anybody anymore without her coming up. They're always like, 'where's Shannon, is she okay?' " Richard ranted.

"It's like everyone expects me to help her in every class, to be her buddy, hold her books, like I'm her Nanny or something? I don't know why people have to be so demanding.

It's not like she needs me there 24/7. She can't walk, it's not like she's completely paralyzed."

Shannon heard some mumbled responses from other male voices. She couldn't pick out who was speaking or what they were saying. She didn't really want to hear any more of what was said, but she couldn't make herself move.

"There are other people in the world worse off than her," she heard Rich continue. "If they can do it all the time, she should be able to, too. I knew things were gonna be different. It's like, she just wants everybody to do everything for her. It's not like she hasn't had to deal with something major before, I mean she..." His words drifted off, like he'd thought better of what he was going to say. There were more non-commital sounds of response from the other boys with Richard, but she recognized Mark and Jason's voices in particular. Realising that the voices were getting louder as they approached jolted Shannon out of her hurt disbelief. She just had enough time to wheel into a small alcove before the group passed by. In the shadows, she dropped her head into her hands and cried bitterly. This was just another thing that she had lost. As the tears fell, she curled into herself, wanting to disappear.

By 3pm the redness in Shannon's eyes had almost faded and she had found a quiet bathroom to fix her makeup, so there were no longer the tell-tale smudges. Looking in the mirror of her compact, she checked one final time before going to wait at the exit for her mum.

When she got to the gate, there was a group of juniors crowding their usual meeting place. Craning her neck to see past them, she spotted the car further down the street. Something made her hesitate as she approached the car. Her mum was sitting in the driver's seat, looking vacantly out the window. For the first time Shay noticed the dark circles under

Evelyn's eyes and the deep frown lines covering her forehead. The idea of trying to deal with her mum's pain, along with her own loss felt like it would overwhelm her. She vowed to do what she could to avoid adding more to her mum's worries. So she attempted to make pleasant small talk and appear positive, while hiding her own fears and frustrations behind her old "captain's got it under control" smile.

Once again Shannon had put on the mask of the cheerful and self-assured leader. This had been her coping strategy during her pregnancy in the summer of her fourth form year. This performance meant keeping those who didn't know her at a distance. If they happened to notice her at all, they would only see the positive front of her facade. For Shannon, it seemed the only way for her to retain any semblance of normalcy. She had expanded on this image when she had moved to the new school after giving birth. Now, just as then, she wanted the concern and worried glances to stop. She needed people to know that she wasn't breakable, and that she didn't need their sympathetic cheer. All Shannon wanted was to be treated the way she had been before her injury. So, each time her accident was brought up or people tried to be sympathetic, she insisted she would get better. How else could she hold onto the fragile hope that things would improve and that she would walk again?

Chapter Eight

Date night had always been special for Shannon. It was the only time in the week where she felt there was someone who she loved, who could see her for who she was, or at least that was how it had been. She still hoped that it was true. This time, the only change to their usual ritual was that rather than Shannon driving to meet Richard, he was coming to pick her up. The situation brought to mind images of old movies where the gentleman collects the lady at her door, showing courtesy and respect. As she waited anxiously, Shannon tried to hold in her mind these images of romance and grace.

Looking at her phone impatiently, she realized it was only 6.15pm. There was still fifteen minutes before she was expecting Rich to arrive. It was hard to keep calm and positive against the sting of Rich's rant that she had overheard, but she was determined to try for a good evening.

Sitting in front of her mum's mirror, Shannon smoothed her beautiful deep blue shirt. Richard had always complimented her whenever she wore it. She went back to wait in the living room, sitting near the window where she could see him arrive.

When Shannon answered the door to Richard's knock,

there was hardly a pause in his greeting before he bent and kissed her on the cheek. "You look great," he commented warmly. "Are you ready to go?" "Sure!" she answered, with a slightly tense smile. "See you later mum!" she called down the hall. "Have a good time... and don't forget to be back by 10pm Shay..." her mother replied.

Getting into Richard's car wasn't hard, now that the process was familiar to Shannon. The rehab workouts were helping her get more of her coordination and strength back. But doing it in front of Richard made her feel clumsy and awkward. Trying to ignore these self-conscious thoughts, she lifted one leg at a time into position and then slid her body across to the car seat.

"I think there are some access parking spots on the side street just up there," Shannon indicated to her right as they drove down the main street. "It's so much easier when there's a wide parking space," she added.

As Richard turned his car into the street, they realized that all the spots were taken. Some were occupied by cars with mobility tags — but there was also a massive trailer, that just seemed to have been left there. "What the... ! I can't believe people can be that inconsiderate," Rich groaned.

"It's okay," Shay said. "I'm sure there will be some other place," she continued in a calm voice.

After Rich had turned the car back onto the street where the restaurant was, they found that all the parking spaces were full with vehicles. When Richard spotted a parallel park just around the corner from the restaurant, he took it without thinking twice.

Getting out of the car, he went to the back passenger door to retrieve Shay's chair. It had fitted in easily enough, but it didn't seem to come back out the same way. After twisting and maneuvering the awkward object for a few minutes, he finally pulled it free of whatever it had been stuck on. Following the simple steps Shay had described at her house for closing the chair, he reversed the process and finally positioned it by her now open door. Richard was feeling a prickle of tension down his back, after the parking issue and wrestling with the damn chair. He just hoped there weren't any further issues, otherwise his attempts to seem like a good boyfriend were going to fail utterly.

"Umm, this is a bit tricky," Shay said hesitantly, indicating the gap created by the gutter which ran between the seat of the car and the chair. "I'm not sure I can get across without falling on my butt," she continued.

Richard's stomach clenched. It seemed like things just weren't going to work out.

"Could you lift me please?" Shay asked, reaching out. "Just pretend you're the knight in shining armour rescuing the fair maid from the tower..." she said, trying to be light-hearted, "... and I'll play the part of the maiden being swept off her feet," she smiled hopefully.

Moving the chair out of the way, Rich furtively looked around to check that there weren't people watching. He didn't really know why, but it didn't feel right that he was doing this, as he stepped forward and put his arms around Shay. The situation felt like it was something too intimate, even though they were boyfriend and girlfriend, like he could be accused of doing something inappropriate.

When they entered the restaurant, it seemed to be particularly busy. They were greeted by a waiter at the door, asking for their reservation name. "Richard Martens, for two," Richard responded. "Oh... you might need to give us a few minutes to arrange a table with more space. Unfortunately because we're so busy, things are more crowded than usual," replied the waiter. Richard felt that he had stuffed up yet again. "How did I forget to check the setup here?" he thought to himself. But luckily it didn't take long for them to be seated and start considering the menu.

"So, how is the Winter Ball dance committee going?" asked Shannon, looking over her menu. "I saw you talking with Nicky the other day, but I haven't been able to catch up with her yet," she continued, struggling for conversation topics.

"It's been going all right... Nicky said they have it under control, only a few dramas with permits and stuff, but they're all good now. She was playing up the fact that she had to pretty much sign her soul over to the Principal and Chairperson of the PTA to get the go ahead for the lighting setup at the entrance. I'm pretty sure everyone can see through her exaggeration. She just likes to be seen as the martyr." He joked, stopping to take a drink of water.

"Hey!" he continued, his face brightening. "Remember after last Ball, when we went with Nick and Sarah and snuck into her neighbours heated pool and went skinny dipping? That was such a rush. I can't believe we almost got caught!"

Shannon smiled half-heartedly, feeling like those days were another lifetime ago. "Yeah, that was a great night..."

Both Shannon and Rich turned their attention to their food when it arrived. It was a welcome distraction to their somewhat uneasy conversation. The plates in front of each of them were like artworks of vegetables and other edibles, which had been cut, shaped and arranged in a way that seemed to add to the deliciousness. As they both slowly ate their way through the masterpieces, they mainly talked about the food and the restaurant around them. At one of the pauses in eating, Shannon noticed a couple walk in wrapped in each other's arms. She watched them covertly as they were directed to their seats. She felt a tear prickle at her eye as she saw the man assist his partner into her seat and brush a kiss to her cheek before he took his own seat. This scene of easy affection really made her feel the difference in the atmosphere between herself and Richard.

"So... who are you going to take to the dance this year?" she asked, wondering how he would respond. It seemed like now was the time to figure out how things really were.

"What! Aren't we going together?" he asked, puzzled by the question, which seemed to come out of nowhere.

"No, I don't think so," she responded bluntly. "I'm not going to be back to dancing that soon, and you know I probably couldn't get to wherever the after party was anyway..." she said, trailing off.

She thought about the conversation she had overheard Richard having with his friends. "I mean, I probably don't want to go anyways. It wouldn't be as fun for me. You should go with someone else, so you can see how everything turned out," she offered.

"What, why would I go with someone else? You're my girlfriend." He reached over to take her hand. "I love you. I don't want to go with anyone else." His tone was full of sincerity.

Shannon was confused by his response. She couldn't decide if she was pleased or annoyed that he was holding on like this. "Well, I don't know why you would want to go with someone who seems to demand so much from you and expect to be looked after 24/7," she responded with an eyebrow raised in challenge, as she withdrew her hand from his.

"Oh no. You heard that?" Richards face scrunched up in distress.

"Yes, I heard. I can't believe you would break my trust like that. You didn't just whine to your friends about how I'm so needy and how you're embarrassed to be with me, but you nearly told them about Louise," she finished in an angry whisper.

"Look, I'm really sorry. I was angry and I just sort of let it slip. It's not like this hasn't been hard on me."

"Right, like I'm not dealing with anything either?" Shannon snapped in response, fighting to keep her voice low. "If you can't handle where I'm at, then we are obviously both better off alone."

"I can't believe you think that, I mean, we have been through so much together," he responded, sounding distressed.

"Well that's all fine, but it's obviously not enough for you, if you can say all those things to your friends," she said in a hurt voice. "Stop pretending. You need to be honest."

"But... Umm. Yeah, okay, maybe you're right..." His voice was low and defeated. "I should have been honest with you... I'm not coping." He sighed, running his hands through his hair again in agitation. "I should have been more upfront with you... I'm really sorry and I don't want this to happen, but if you want we could take a break."

Shannon pressed her palms to her eyes, trying to prevent the stinging tears that threatened. "This isn't just a break, Rich. This is final. It's not fair to either of us, to think this is going to work out." Her voice cracked on the last word and she broke down, letting some tears escape.

The rest of the meal continued in a heavy silence. Both Rich and Shannon struggled to keep their emotions in check as they left the restaurant and returned to the car. Reaching the curb, they both realized they still had to deal with the awkward transfer back into the car in order to get home.

After opening the door, Richard gently picked Shannon up. With his arm wrapped around her shoulders and his other arm tucked under her knees, they were drawn close to each other. The brush of her hair against his shoulder stirred up the smell of the floral sweet shampoo that she had always used. It was the worst kind of wrench, to have to pull away from her familiar warmth and scent, knowing it was probably the last time they would willingly have such contact. Stepping back as quickly as possible, Rich packed the chair away before taking the driver's seat.

When the car pulled up outside Shannon's house and her chair stood waiting for her, Richard waited off to the side. As she wheeled toward the house, Rich followed close by. When she reached the door he stopped her with a light hand on her shoulder. "Look Shay, I really am sorry." He gently took her hand and kissed her knuckles. "Bye," he said, leaving with his head down.

Chapter Nine

The bell startled Shay, disrupting her thoughts. The loud screech of chairs being shifted alerted her to the fact it was lunchtime. Sighing, she wheeled towards the door.

"Shannon — can I talk to you for a minute please?"

Shay paused, slowly turning to face Mrs Jones at the whiteboard.

In the back of the class Rich froze in a crouch, his arm poised, fingers grasping his loose sketches that had fallen to the floor during the end of class rush. He found himself unable to move when he overheard Mrs Jones call out to Shannon. Despite his brain demanding he run away, his muscles remained unresponsive.

"Umm, of course..." Her eyes quickly scanned the empty classroom.

Reassured, but with her pulse racing, Shannon sat, her hands awkwardly fiddling with her sleeve buttons. "I've noticed you've become a little distracted and irritable, are you feeling okay?" "Umm... yeah I guess..." she sighed, avoiding eye contact. "Before the accident things weren't perfect, but I had friends... conversations... people could relate to me. I know things are different now, but it's even harder for me when everyone's treating me like I'm some fragile ornament... or some alien." Colour rushed to Shay's cheeks. She continued, with the frown deepening, "I just don't know how to get everyone to treat me the way they used to."

Horror and guilt consumed Rich as he listened to Shay's admission. An onslaught of memories assaulted him: his big brother Tim and his mates, the ever-present sounds of laughter and joking, mucking around in the back yard with a ball, talking him through shooting his first ever three-pointer under their hoop at home.

Another memory invaded his mind: the piercing sound of the phone, their mother's cries of distress. Later, the sharp unpleasant scents of the hospital stung his nostrils, Tim unresponsive and broken on the bed.

The similarities to Shay's situation slapped him in the face. After Tim was discharged, his friends had been noticeable by their absence. His brother had become dependent and vulnerable; no longer could Rich rely on him for guidance. His hero had vanished and left behind a damaged and withdrawn individual he could no longer recognise.

Shay paused, watching Mrs Jones's rhythmic arm movements as she wiped the board clear before she set the duster down and turned her gaze back to her student.

"Thanks for being honest, Shannon. It's often hard for people to accept change, but sometimes it's easier to have understanding with a little information... Give me 'til tomorrow and I'll get back to you with an idea that might help the situation."

Silence greeted Rich as he eventually broke free of the grip the memories had taken on him. His shaky legs carried him back to a chair, where he collapsed, overwhelmed and dazed.

Next morning Shay found herself in Mrs Jones's class again, anxiously awaiting her teacher's bright idea.

"Alright people, your attention this way, thank you... I have a new assignment for you all." Mrs Jones directed a brief reassuring smile to Shannon. Shay caught her breath. "How does an extra assignment help my situation?" she wondered.

"This assignment, to be completed in two weeks, requires you to prepare a verbal report on a significant, life changing event that has happened to you."

A rush of disappointed sighs echoed in the room.

"You'll present the content of your report to the class, detailing what this event was, how it has affected how others see you and also, how you see yourself. This report ties in with our reflective/personal writing module, see your updated assignment schedule," she instructed, as she handed out papers.

"Oh, I've got this. Junior Sportsman of the year." A confident voice spoke up, followed by a chuckle.

"When my baby sister was born!" came another excited whisper.

While most people in the class talked excitedly, Shannon sat stiff and silent, thinking. "Oh no, this is seriously not what I want to deal with right now! Talk about being thrown in the deep end." She prayed the period bell would hurry up and ring, so she could escape to deal with her panic. She was not expecting this. Her chest burned, as she realized the ball was now in her court. This was her opportunity to bring about the change she wanted — and it was an overwhelming prospect.

Chapter Ten

The music carried Tim's thoughts, as he watched shrubs moving in the wind, seemingly keeping rhythm. A slow smile spread, the only indication of life in an otherwise still being. In the background, a movement caught his eye and prompted him to reduce the volume. Rich sidled over to his big brother.

"Hey. Sup?"

"Hey, you're home early. How was school?"

"Oh, you know. Same old. How was your day?"

Pursed lips grew into a grin. "Oh you know. Achieving world peace, saved the polar bears. Same old." That old twinkle flashed at Rich, sparking the realisation that his brother was still the same. Rich wondered how many times this had gone unnoticed. He felt his shoulders relaxing as he slouched back into the couch.

"Wow. Sounds better than mine, the teachers are all harping on about exam preparation... in between all the girls of course"

A quiet chuckle broke through the silence that for the first time in a long while sat comfortably between them. Richard realized that it was the first time in ages that he had felt close to Tim.

Chapter Eleven

With everything else swimming around in the agitated and murky pools of her mind, social status had become almost meaningless to Shannon. It was just too hard to think about reputation, when she had to put most of her effort into keeping up a front of resigned happiness. Her social standing wasn't priority number one anymore. Just having a couple of good friends right now would do fine. Caught up in thought, Shannon was oblivious to Koro Artie's whistling, until the impact of small objects repeatedly landing on her face demanded her attention. The whistling was replaced by hoots of laughter.

"Geez girl, did the fairies pinch your brain this arvo?"

"Huh?" A small pile of seed pods was sitting in her lap.

"Come on over. I've got something to show you." A newly built gate swung open and Koro Artie appeared, overalls and boots covered in dust.

Taken aback, Shannon grinned. "Whoa, what the... when did you?"

"Well, I could've done the whole thing this afternoon with you sitting right there, and you wouldn't have even noticed me, you're that far away in dream land!"

On the far side of the yard the door to Koro's workshop stood ajar, the leg of an upright easel visible from outside. "Come on – I've got a new piece to show you."

The old workshop door screeched loudly in protest as Koro pulled it open further.

Shannon gazed at the painting on display. It was the portrait of a young Maori woman. She was wearing a mix of European and traditional clothing. In the background of the painting there were shadowy figures disappearing into the depths of the picture. At first they seemed like reflections of the central figure, but when she looked closer she could see that there were slight differences, she could pick out some of the shadows as being male or female.

"What do you think, ne kotiro?" Koro's voice pulled Shannon's attention away from the painting.

"It's beautiful, the details of the woman are amazing," she answered truthfully.

"I'm glad you like it." He turned away with a pleased smile and started talking to her about other pieces of art that were leaning here and there against the walls or standing on drying racks.

Shannon only half listened as her eyes roamed across the paintings lining the walls and stacked in piles everywhere. Even though the space was so full of beautiful pieces and curious artworks and odd items, it didn't seem crowded. She could smell a mixture of paint and warm dust, as she watched the autumn light filtering in through the various windows. An old chest at the back of the room caught her eye. It reminded her of the treasure chests in pirate stories from her childhood.

"What's that?" she finally asked, pointing to it.

"Oh, that old thing? Actually it's been so long since I looked inside, I don't even remember! Hang on..." A small chuckle escaped Koro's lips and he turned towards Shannon. "Come look."

Dodging easel legs and paint supplies, Shay wheeled across, peering over the top edge of the box as Koro Artie pushed back the lid. "This was my first set of chisels. From when I was a young fullah. Bit rusty, eh."

Shannon watched eagerly as he laid out the leather roll. Only the worn and scratched handles of the tools were visible.

"Chisels? What did you have chisels for?" she asked with curiosity. "I thought you've always painted?"

"Well, for the past 40 years I have. But before that, I was a bit of an up and coming boatwright."

"Huh? Boat what?"

"Hurrumph! A boatwright. Can't just make a boat by waving a magic wand like those fairy friends of yours!" Koro Artie slowly pulled out a dented and faded tin box, flicking it open with his thumb. "Aaahhh... haven't seen these beauties in a while." In his hand he held black and white photos. Shay strained her neck trying to see them.

"Ahem," she muttered.

"Oh sorry girl — here, come over here," he motioned, sitting down on a pile of old boxes in the corner.

"See this boat? Oh, she was a beauty. My first boat I ever helped craft. Aaahhh, 32 foot, all native timber you know. Most of that wood came from down the line, shipped up to Whaingaroa. I loved being an apprentice. Some of the best years of my life before my accident, see. I thought it was all over you know, losing my forearm and elbow. The nightmares were the worst, I used to relive that day over and over..."

A sympathetic shiver passed through Shay's body as she absorbed his words.

"Even though my family supported me, they were hard

times, and not being able to pull my weight and help out at home was no good... so I just had to get up and find a way to get things done.

"It was bloody hard, and people weren't easy on me just because I'd lost my arm. Everyone still expected me to do my bit, after I got my head around it all. There was this one uncle, who sat me down about a month after I came back home. He said, 'Boy, you can't expect everyone to keep carrying you. You lost your arm, not your brain or your gifts. You have a lot to give yet, and by crikey your whanau still need you to help out.'

So eventually I started pulling myself back together, looking ahead and trying to get on with things the best I could."

Shay shifted uneasily in her chair.

"Koro, do you paint with water colours as well?"

Koro Artie paused, slowly realising the reason for Shay changing the subject.

"Well... no, no I don't. Hey, you know what I feel like right now? A tall glass of cold lemon and barley, I brought some out earlier. Come on, let's go sit under the trees."

Chapter Twelve

Knock, knock. Shannon had spent the morning waiting for that sound with a mix of anticipation and dread. She had fretted restlessly about everything, from her outfit choice to the number of cushions on the sofa. It seemed like such a silly thing to be getting uptight about, but today Katey was coming, the first of Shannon's school friends to visit since the accident.

Shannon kept thinking anxiously through all the possible ways the afternoon could turn out. Good, bad, and everything in between. At last, the doorbell rang. "I'll get it!" she called down the hall. Awkwardly manoeuvring her chair, she reached across to turn the door handle and slowly reversed away to swing the door wide to receive her visitor. Standing outside, with a backpack slung over one shoulder and a box of chocolates in her hand, was Katey.

"Hey, great to see you!" she greeted Shannon with a friendly and open smile.

"Put your things on the sofa," Shannon said. "I'll just check on the popcorn."

Katey sniffed the air as they made their way into the kitchen. "If someone figured out how to bottle that fresh popcorn smell they'd make a fortune," she joked.

"I brought a whole bunch of movies with me, I wasn't sure what you'd feel like watching. There's couple of rom-coms, American Pie, and I even snuck one of my brother's horror flicks if you feel like being scared." she rattled on, ticking off the list on her fingers.

Shannon found herself easily falling into conversation with Katey as they debated the various movie choices. The microwave beeped, signalling that their popcorn was ready.

Rolling across the kitchen, Shannon reached up to retrieve the bag of light and fluffy popcorn, but as she grasped the bag she realised it was much hotter than expected.

"Ouch ouch ouch!" she cried, snatching her hand back and knocking the bag of popcorn onto the floor. Before she could react, Katey quickly reached down and collected the still sealed bag, holding it gingerly by one corner. "You could have warned me you wanted to play hot potato," she said, grinning. "I may be a netball player, but I'm not great at spontaneous coordination."

Carefully placing the popcorn bag on the kitchen bench, Katey looked across at Shannon, who sat cradling her stinging hand.

"Do you want me to put this into that dish?" she gestured to the bowl that stood on the bench.

As Katey helped set out the popcorn and drinks, Shannon began to relax. She stopped being so stressed about her own clumsiness. The two girls easily worked together as a team, with Katey collecting items from various shelves and places in the kitchen that Shannon couldn't reach easily. "We can put everything on a tray — I think there's one in the cupboard above the fridge," Shannon said. "I'm still working out where Mum keeps some things."

She was even relaxed enough that she didn't get too upset when the DVD wouldn't start.

"I'm sorry Katey, I don't know why this stupid machine isn't working," she said, poking irritably at the buttons of the unresponsive DVD player. "Sorry to have wasted your time.

"Don't worry, we can watch movies another time," Katey responded with an easy smile. "I have some YouTube clips to show you, if I can use your laptop? There are some really funny cat videos I found the other night, and some others showing amazing magic tricks... Honestly, I waste so much time on YouTube!"

After eating and laughing their way through countless videos, they found themselves on a series of hair and makeup tutorials.

"Wow, look at that one!" Katey said, pointing to an intricate braided hairstyle. "How about we try out some of these, you have such nice hair Shay, and I haven't seen you do anything exciting with it in ages. Those different braids and things you used to do with your hair were so cool."

"Yeah, that sounds like a great idea," said Shannon. "I guess it has been ages since I have worried about my hair." They spent some more time scrolling through hair tutorials and decided to try out the Milkmaid Braid.

Minutes into their efforts at trying to recreate the hairstyle according to the tutorial, Katey was struggling with her fine blonde flyaway hair. "My fringe keeps falling out of the braid. This is so annoying," she huffed.

"Here, you need to separate the fringe before you start! Let me help you with that side," offered Shannon, reaching across to grab her parting comb. When Shannon had finished fixing up Katey's troublesome hair, she sent her off to look in the bathroom mirror.

"Wow! I look good!" Katey laughed. "You are definitely going to have to show me how to do this. It shows off my new highlights so well. Do you want some help pinning up yours? You have so much hair, I'm jealous!" she offered as she entered back into the room.

"Yeah, sure!" replied Shannon.

Grabbing some clips off the dresser, Katey proceeded to pin Shannon's thick jet black braids in place. It was a fun afternoon for both girls, and Shannon realised how much she'd missed spending time with her friend.

By five o'clock both Katey and Shannon had had enough hairstyling, makeovers and manicures. They sat on the sofa in the living room, flicking through some magazines that Shannon's mum had bought.

"You know," Katey said, closing her magazine in her lap, "I really liked your speech the other day in English. I mean, it was so cool to actually understand something of what this new thing," she waved at the chair, "is like for you. From what some of the others were saying, they didn't have any idea that they were being so clueless. I think they were pretty much ready to start making an apology card or something."

"I really didn't like doing that presentation," Shannon said. "I'm not much of a fan of having a room full of people watching me."

"Yeah, I don't really like the spotlight much either, but you did such a good job. I feel like you got your point across really well," Katey spoke sincerely. Checking her phone for the time, she sighed.

"Oh, I better get going, mum and dad are picky about having me home to help make dinner. It's been really fun hanging out. Hopefully next time we can see a movie as well?"

As she got up from the couch, Katey reached over and

wrapped her arms around Shannon in a friendly hug. "See you Monday," she said on her way out the door.

"Hold on," Shannon said. "I'll come out with you to your car." As Katey watched from the doorway, Shannon shifted her chair into place and manoeuvred herself back to the seat. Following Katey down the ramp to the driveway, she saw Koro walking along the street. As they neared the car, the old man caught Shannon's eye and waved cheerfully at her. Smiling, she returned the wave.

"This is my friend Katey," she called to him. Following Shay's gaze, Katey waved in greeting as well.

Opening the car door, Katey got into her seat. "I had a good time," she said. "Catch you at school."

As Shannon turned to wheel back inside, she realised with surprise how unselfconscious she had felt throughout the afternoon. Even though things had started with nerves and some awkwardness, it had all worked out well.

Chapter Thirteen

At school the following week, Katey and a couple of Shannon's old netball teammates sat with Shannon under a shady tree.

"So what's the plan for this fun game between us and Tyson's?" Rachael asked.

"It's $2 per ticket to raise money for the primary school's playground," Katey replied. "If we try our luck with the teachers and our friends and family we should do all right. We need to get a good crowd to cheer us against those loud Tyson supporters... they're intense."

"We better not give them too many reasons to cheer then! We can't let those old girls beat us," Sarah laughed. "Millie won't let us live it down if her team wins."

Rach smirked at Sarah. "Well, you best have 100% shooting stats then."

"Only if you don't pass away any turnover ball," Sarah replied, laughing.

As Katey and her teammates discussed strategy and compared the two teams' players, Shannon stayed out of the conversation at first, feeling sad that she wouldn't be playing. But when the others started arguing over whether man on man defence versus zone defence gave the better competitive advantage against the Tyson players, she couldn't help throwing in her own opinion. It didn't take long before she was heatedly discussing the rest of the game plans that the girls were considering taking to the team.

The excitement of working out tactics and contributing to the direction of the team was really uplifting for Shannon. When the other girls encouraged her to come along to the game, she didn't hesitate to say yes.

On the afternoon of the match Shannon was sitting on the sidelines with a group of other fans, all wearing school colours in support of the team. The whistle signalled the start of the game, and Shannon felt the familiar adrenaline building up. As the game progressed, along with the raised voices of the other supporters, she became more and more animated, yelling at lost turnover ball, and cheering when Rachael came out flying for an intercept. Watching her old teammates passing the ball confidently, and the quick change of direction in the set plays around the court, was so familiar that Shannon almost felt she was part of the action.

Chapter Fourteen

The call from the spinal clinic had been a surprise. They rarely contacted Shannon or her mum, other than sending letters about support groups and review schedules. When Evelyn came to her with a nervous and half-hoping smile, Shannon felt her stomach flip in nervous expectation. Trying to pretend she hadn't heard part of the brief call, she asked, "What was that about?" "That was the clinic... They want to see us on Wednesday morning," her mum replied, still smiling.

Sitting in the busy waiting room of the spinal clinic was an exercise in control. "How long do you think we'll have to wait?" Shannon asked at the front desk, looking around at the bustling seating area. "I was told to be here for my appointment at 11.15am, but it looks like there are so many others waiting." The receptionist replied with a smile, "We are rather busy today, but don't worry, there are multiple doctors and clinics working from this area, so I'm sure you'll be seen soon."

By the time Shay was called to the specialist's office she was a ball of nervous excitement. All the therapy sessions and exercises were hard, but she had been making so much effort, and the therapy assistants were always so supportive and positive. It gave Shannon a sense of hope that the doctor might have some exciting news from the last set of tests. "It's nice to see you, Shannon and Mrs Carlisle. Thank you for coming in today," Dr Metris greeted them, as he took his seat at the desk. "The reports I've received from the therapists say you have been attending regularly and doing very well with your physical strength training and movement exercises," he smiled.

Shannon reached over and took her mum's hand, squeezing it in anticipation.

"Shall we start with you giving me an update on how you feel you've been doing, Shannon...?"

While Shannon talked, she noticed that her doctor continued to nod and smile encouragingly, as he scribbled down notes on the file in front of him. It felt like further confirmation that she would be going home with good news. Even if it meant more months of hard training to get walking again, she would commit in a heartbeat. She felt that she had already shown she was more than capable of hard work when it came to goals, so that was no concern.

"That sounds fantastic, Shannon, it seems that you have been doing very well." Dr Metris stopped and cleared his throat. "There is however something I need to make sure you understand at this point... something you seem unclear about. In my opinion, based on the results from your therapy and other tests, I'm sad to say that it isn't going to be possible for you to regain use of your legs."

Everything in Shannon's world ground to a halt. Although she could see the doctor's mouth moving, she couldn't make sense of any words. It seemed as though everything had become numb, her senses no longer able to decipher the messages they were receiving. The warm presence of her mum's arm wrapped around her shoulder, and the gentle but firm squeezing of their clasped hands, was a reassuring anchor in the haze that had fallen on her. Turning to see her mum's face, Shannon could see her talking with the doctor. She knew questions were being asked and answered, but she couldn't process the details.

When the doctor stood to open the door for them to exit the office, Shannon regained some of her senses, and she reached to propel herself from the room. By this time it was an instinct to reach for her wheels, before her mum or anyone else could offer to help.

Reaching the privacy of the car in the huge parking block, Shannon felt herself beginning to shake. The initial numbing shock of the doctor's announcement was wearing off and the implications were sinking in. Tears poured forth, coming out in deep shaking sobs.

For a moment Evelyn sat in silence, before reaching out and wrapping Shannon in a tight hug, rocking their bodies side to side in imitation of the way she held her as a baby.

"Don't worry honey, it's okay to cry, you have been so strong through everything," she soothed. Evelyn continued to hold and rock her daughter as she fell apart in her arms. She could see that Shay was finally letting go, and Evelyn wanted to prove that she was capable of being there and supporting her daughter, in ways she hadn't been in the past.

No longer able to deny the finality of her situation, Shay fell into a deep sadness, feeling like she was surrounded by thick cotton wool. Everything around her seemed unclear and unimportant. People who talked to her just sounded like a mumbling annoyance. Everything took so much more effort, including maintaining her commitment to the exercise and rehab sessions, which had previously been so important. The doctor's definite diagnosis had changed everything for her. Now all this effort seemed pointless.

Each time she came home from physical therapy and there was no change, it was just another confirmation of the diagnosis. Sometimes she would cry till her eyes burned and turned a dull scarlet. It relieved her somewhat, to pour out every hopeless feeling with each chocked sob, and then, when she couldn't force out another tear, she'd fall into a dreamless sleep. Other times she would bury her face in her blankets and scream, beating her pillow in frustration. Those feelings of being on top of the world and in control were gone. The memories of those times when everything was so quick and easy burned in her heart as she tried to deal with the loss. Her counsellor said all of this was perfectly natural and would pass, that it was just part of the mourning process. But Shannon couldn't believe that she would ever feel okay again.

Chapter Fifteen

Evelyn stood in Shannon's doorway, looking at the lumpy pile of bedcovers and pillows.

"Honey? It's time to go to your exercise session. We need to hurry or we'll be late."

"I don't want to go!" came the muffled reply from the bed.

"But honey, these sessions are supposed to help..." Evelyn said, stepping over to the bed and perching on the edge.

"Nothing will help," wailed Shannon. "I won't ever walk again... Just leave me alone."

"But..." Evelyn tried again. "No," Shannon said firmly. "Just. Leave. Me. Alone!" she shouted from under the covers.

Evelyn's shoulders slumped, and she sighed. "You know what?" she said, her voice cracking, "maybe you're right. Maybe you'd be just as miserable out there as in here." She stood looking at her daughter, tears stinging her eyes, before walking away.

Several hours later, Evelyn was still trying to think what to do about Shannon. The house was noisy and full of tradesmen, building ramps and other accommodations for Shannon. Looking out the back window, she could see the portable ramp leaning against the fence to make space for the new permanent ramp. As Evelyn was staring at the piles of wood and equipment, she saw the man who Shannon called Koro, working in his back garden. Evelyn knew that he had given comfort and encouragement to Shannon. Maybe he would have some advice for Evelyn.

Stepping back down the hallway, she stopped and listened outside Shannon's door. It was hard to hear anything over the noise being made by the builders. Quietly, Evelyn opened the bedroom door just enough to peer in and see the slow rise and fall of her daughter's breathing as she slept. It was bewildering that even in her emotional state Shannon could sleep through the noise, but at least when Shannon was asleep she was at peace, Evelyn thought to herself. Comforted by this thought, she went out into the back garden in search of guidance.

As Evelyn approached the back fence, Koro Artie called out a friendly greeting. Evelyn smiled in return. She had been watching her daughter's interactions with their neighbour from a distance, but had only spoken with the elderly man once or twice, very briefly.

"Hello there," she greeted him now. "I wondered if you have a few minutes for a chat...?"

"Come on over and have a cuppa," he replied, waving her toward the kitchen door.

Evelyn stepped through the gap in the fence that Shannon had gone through so many times, and followed the old man into his house.

"Come in and take a seat." Koro stepped back back from the door and waved her over to the table, before turning to the kettle and cups on his kitchen bench. "Do you want milk or sugar with your tea, ne kotiro?"

Evelyn sat stirring her drink thoughtfully. The warm atmosphere of her neighbour's 1970s kitchen, with its brown laminate countertops and netting curtains, was both comforting and unsettling. It brought up many memories for her. So many key events in her life had taken place around kitchen tables not unlike this one. Happy childhood memories, mixed with less pleasant episodes from her teen years, and then she recalled another kitchen, where she sat with Shannon's father in their early happy months after they eloped.

Her thoughts were interrupted by Koro's gentle question: "How are you and the young one doing? I haven't seen her about for a few days. I thought perhaps she might be away visiting family or something." Koro's words stopped when he saw Evelyn shake her head.

"No, she's had some bad news from the doctors." Evelyn said sadly. "He told us that she won't be able to walk again... It was such a shock, especially for Shay... She really thought she would be able to walk again in time." Evelyn's voice broke, as tears trickled down her cheeks. "She's put so much effort in, and she's been through so much... she's always been such a strong person, even when she was younger. Now it seems like she's lost all her fight. She won't try anything; she hardly even gets out of bed and barely touches her meals. I don't know how to reach her. Every time I try to get her to talk she tells me to leave her alone."

Koro reached into his pocket and took out a clean handkerchief. "It's good that she has your support, and that you keep making the effort," he said. Handing the hanky to Evelyn, he asked her, "What do you think is the difference between what she pulled through when she was younger, and what she is going through now?"

"It's a long complicated story," Evelyn replied, dabbing at her eyes. "She dealt with a lot, more than I realized at the time.

You see, her dad and I were still happy together till she was thirteen or so, but then things started getting more and more difficult between us."

Her mind brought up images of a younger Shannon, with her hair loose, dressed in her navy uniform, heading to school with a group of friends.

"And then towards the end of that year, things really hit the wall for her dad and I. We spent so much time arguing and when we weren't, I was so preoccupied with trying to keep the peace. I guess it really wasn't the kind of space a kid wants to be in."

An image of Shannon's closed bedroom door, with loud music coming from behind it, appeared in Evelyn's mind.

"I wasn't always even sure if she was at home when she was supposed to be. I'm ashamed to admit that. Shannon tended to shut herself away and play music to drown us out. I mean, I would have, if it had been me." Evelyn paused, wiped her eyes and took a sip of sweet tea.

"So you are saying, you feel that Shay was affected by your conflict with her father?" Koro asked.

"She wasn't just hiding away in her room to avoid what was going on." Evelyn's voice cracked. "She told me years later that she'd started sneaking out with friends, drinking, going to parties... and she... started seeing an older boy from her school... She went out with him one night after things had been particularly bad at home, and she ended up getting pregnant..."

"I see," Koro said quietly.

"I had no idea. It was a real shock when I got a call from Shannon's gym teacher saying that she had been hassled by the other girls for getting fat. When the teacher spoke to Shannon, she realised what was going on. I didn't believe it at first, but when they sent Shay home and we talked, she told me that she had been hiding her baby bump for weeks, hoping it would disappear. It was then that I realized how preoccupied I'd been. Not even noticing those changes in my own daughter... That's when I knew things had to change. I made sure Shay came first, from that point forward."

Evelyn paused, and Koro exhaled slowly. "Did the baby survive?"

"Yes, she did." Evelyn spoke with a small smile. "A beautiful little girl. Shay wanted to call her Louise, after a favourite storybook character. But we both realised as her pregnancy continued that she just couldn't keep the baby at such a young age. I didn't want her to repeat my mistakes, but it seems they happened anyhow."

"So you gave the child away?"

"Yes. An aunt that I had stayed in contact with... she was the only family member who still talked to me, she helped me to find a good family. A distant cousin who didn't know my story and wasn't going to judge Shay as a result. It really was hard for both of us to give up our flesh and blood, but it was the best thing to do for the baby and Shannon. At least my aunt occasionally sends a photo and a little note."

"That's at least some reassurance for you both," Koro said. "But what about the father?"

"When Shannon told the young man who got her pregnant, he called her a liar and refused to talk to her again. Just like her own dad, when the passion and fun was over he didn't want to be around anymore. I guess the fantasies her dad and I had created of grand adventures and traveling the world didn't live up to the pressures of making a living and having a child to feed... Don't get me wrong, I'm sure Shannon's dad loved her, but things got so poisonous between us that he left. We were going to have kids, someday, but having Shannon wasn't what we had expected so soon after we eloped. We were just kids ourselves. I feel so horrible that my choices have meant that Shay doesn't have a father or grandparents, and sometimes I feel like she hasn't even had a mother..."

Evelyn broke down into heavy sobs, resting her head on her arms and leaning onto the table. Koro reached over and placed a reassuring hand on her arm.

After a few minutes of quiet, interrupted by Evelyn's weeping and ragged breaths, Koro spoke again. "I can understand you're feeling bad about what's happened in the past, but think about what you're doing now. You're not running away from this problem, you're standing right there beside your girl. All you can do sometimes when things get rough is keep bailing out the boat until the waters calm and you can start moving again. That's what Shannon needs right now, and that's what you're giving her. And just remember, neither of you are doing it alone."

When Evelyn finally stopped crying, she sat up and wiped her eyes. Looking at the older man, she smiled.

"Thank you... I feel like I have been carrying that story around with me like a tonne of bricks. You are so lovely for listening to me babble on, and for being so supportive to Shay."

Koro smiled in return. When Evelyn stood to leave he followed. As she reached the doorway, Evelyn turned and wrapped the older man in a hug.

"Thank you," she repeated.

"You're welcome child, just remember, you and your girl aren't in this alone. There are people all around willing to help, if they only know you need it." He patted her back gently.

Evelyn felt a new strength after the conversation with Koro.

It had lifted a weight off her shoulders, allowing her to put more focus into being there for Shay.

Chapter Sixteen

As Evelyn was folding washing in the living room, she heard steps approaching on the ramp, followed by a knock at the door. She was surprised to see Katey and several other teenagers she recognised from sports games and school events.

"Hi Mrs Carlisle, we were hoping to see Shay," Katey said. "She was supposed to be at the student council meeting earlier today. We're making the final vote on next year's student member for the board of trustees."

One of the boys spoke: "Since she didn't turn up, we thought we would drop in and get her input... our vote is tied at the moment." Evelyn recognised him, but couldn't put a name to his face.

"Just wait here a minute, I'll see what Shannon is up to." She turned down the hallway feeling apprehensive, unsure of Shannon's response to her classmates' unexpected arrival.

Lying under the covers, Shannon heard the knock at the door and the voices that followed. With a dull sense of worry, she recognised Katey's voice, and then Sam's. The last time she'd spoken to Sam was the previous week's student council meeting. The details of normal life had been so foggy since the doctor's visit. Part of Shannon's mind wanted to stay curled up and hidden away, another part was prodding her to attend to her responsibilities to the group. By the time she heard her mum in the hallway, she was pushing back the covers and reaching for some clothes.

"I'm coming, just give me a minute." Getting into her clothes was a struggle, everything felt stiff and awkward after several days of inactivity.

"Coming!" she called, as she dragged a brush through her hair, pulling it back into a scruffy bun, realising that it needed washing, before wheeling down the hall. Shannon was shocked to find the entire student council, lounging around in her living room.

"What are you all doing here?"

Several people started to answer at once, all stopped suddenly, then looked at one another before starting again. Shannon glanced around the room, confused about the chaos of voices. She singled out Sam.

"Okay, this isn't working; Sam, can you give me an answer?"

"Yeah, we need your vote as the decider for the student rep for next year. We've narrowed it down to finalists, but can't agree, so we need your input."

"Katey said she hadn't seen you at school, so we figured we'd drop by after your no-show at the meeting and see if you were home," Rachael piped up, "I never really realised how crazy organising stuff was without your input. I mean, we know what we're doing, but agreeing as a group has been impossible."

There was a general murmur of agreement throughout the room.

Shannon took a minute to focus her thoughts. It was a surprise to know that they valued her input so much. This realisation helped to make the smile on her face more genuine. After some time hearing about the candidates and having everyone share their opinions, the group was eventually able to make a choice.

After the meeting was over, and the council had left, Shannon sat in the living room, looking dazed.

"How did that go?"

Shannon's eyes blinked back into focus. "Yeah, it was good. I really had forgotten about the candidate vote this week... I should make sure I haven't forgotten anything else. It's kind of nice to think that you're valued and needed in some way."

Evelyn smiled. "I'm glad the group got an answer. Let me know if you need to get to any other meetings outside of school." Evelyn watched Shannon reaching for her phone, obviously intent on reconnecting with her school life.

Chapter Seventeen

Feeling like there was a lead weight in her stomach, Shannon packed her school books into her bag. "This shouldn't be such a big deal. Why am I freaking out so much?" she said to herself. It just felt weird to be going back to school after being away for the second time this year.

Even though this absence hadn't been anything like as long as the first, Shannon still had that old feeling of being the new kid, the odd one out. Last time she had been worried about being rejected and having to struggle to get around. But it had been a lot better than she had expected.

She told herself that she needed to remember this. At least now she had a better sense of who she was and where she fitted in.

"My name is Shannon Carlisle, I am a student leader, I have friends and family, and I use a wheelchair." Her counsellor had suggested Shannon repeat these words to herself. It was a way of positively reinforcing her condition. The wheelchair was not who she was, but merely a new aspect.

Settling in back at school took some time, but Shannon realised that being there was in many ways a good thing. It gave her things to focus on, and put her in situations where she had to be sociable. It wasn't that she preferred not to socialize, in fact usually the opposite was true. When the sadness, and what the counsellor talked about as grief, had swallowed her up, it had happened so quickly. But climbing back out was surprisingly slow. Although Shannon returned to school with determination, the hazy sadness still lingered. She tried to follow the counsellor's advice of taking one day at a time.

Chapter Eighteen

The music at the end of Moulin Rouge woke Richard up from the haze that he had been in during the last part of the film. It wasn't his idea of a fun movie — he would have preferred *The Shawshank Redemption*, but the boys had been out-voted. Looking around in the darkened classroom, he saw some of the girls dabbing their eyes. When his eyes fell on Shannon, she seemed to be away on some other planet, blankly staring at the screen while tears fell down her cheeks. As the lights came on, he watched her close her eyes. When she opened them again, she wiped the tears from her face and looked around.

"Shay doesn't usually get tearful at sappy movies," Rich thought to himself. It was weird to see a different side of her like this, but it also reminded him of the last time he had seen her cry. Being the cause of those tears still made his stomach twist in guilt.

As the final scene between Ewan McGregor and Nicole Kidman's characters rang out, Shannon felt her breath catch and her eyes overflow with tears. It was so beautiful, but so tragic, that the star-crossed lovers would be separated forever. Her mind drifted along, imagining a happy ending.

When the lights came on, Shannon was jolted out of her

internal movie world. "Wow, that was sad," Rachael leaned over to say.

"Yeah," Shay replied, wiping her eyes and the tear tracks down her cheeks. "It's been ages since I've cried over a movie."

"What did you girls reckon about that?" hissed Sarah, "I fell in love with Ewan McGregor, again, I forgot how hot he is... What do you think about a Ewan McGregor movie marathon in the weekend?"

As the class packed up to move to the next class, Katey came and joined the group of friends talking about movie watching plans. "Am I on the guest list for this movie marathon?" she asked with a smile.

"Totally," they replied.

"Great, I'll see you all at my place at 2pm on Saturday," Rachael confirmed as she picked up her bag.

Shannon took a deep breath and spoke up. "Ahh, just one thing Rach. How will I get into your place? You've got steps, right?"

"Oh yeah, right. Don't worry, we'll sort something," Rachael responded with a smile.

Although she was happy to have plans with her friends, Shannon was still nervous, worrying about how she would get into her friend's house. A few weeks ago, the nerves would have caused her to cancel or to not accept the offer in the first place. But now she was able to get through those moments and actually still want to keep moving and keep trying. She had found a new determination to succeed. She still wasn't sure what this new kind of success looked like, but she wanted to keep going until she could figure things out. The more time she spent with Katey and her other friends, the more she knew that things were getting better.

Chapter Nineteen

The ball had gone by in a blur, with groups of people chatting, posing for photos, and dancing in a crowded and strobe-lit hall. Richard was at the ball with a group of his single guy mates, following through on his breakup agreement with Shannon. Rich and the other guys piled into a large, shiny, 4WD belonging to someone's dad. It had been kind of nice not to be stressing about wearing the right coloured tie, or making a good impression on other parents. The music and atmosphere of the ball helped Richard to have a good time. But by the time things were winding up and people were heading off to after ball parties, he had the beginnings of a headache.

He would have just gone home, but his mates convinced him to go with them to a house party at Mark's place, which was the biggest after ball event.

Sitting on the sofa with a drink in his hand, Richard felt pressure building at the back of his head. It was made worse by the loud music with throbbing bass, and people shouting over the noise. Everyone else seemed to be talking, dancing or getting hot and heavy, like the couple on the sofa next to him. Although pretty much everyone had changed out of their suits or dresses, many people still smelled strongly of colognes and perfumes. This combined with the heat and atmosphere added to his feeling of claustrophobia. Closing his eyes, he tried to zone out, but the longer he waited the worse he felt. It was obvious that the extra drink he had accepted from his mate hadn't been a good idea.

Sliding between the throngs of people, Richard made his way to the front door. The closer he got to the exit, the cooler the air felt. It was a slight relief to the pressure in his head, but now that he was upright, he felt his stomach rolling. He hurried past the last few people, using his elbows to make way. Just as he made it out the door, he lurched to the side of the doorstep and threw up violently into the garden. With an empty stomach, he stood up unsteadily. When the world and his insides had stopped see-sawing, he took shuffling steps towards the street, wanting to put some distance between himself and the noise, but not really knowing where to go.

Making his way down the quiet dark street was a struggle, but Richard just wanted to get some space. He had been trying to feel all right, and there were days where he could admit that he did feel almost normal again. But tonight wasn't one of those times.

Passing quiet gardens and seeing the occasional dimly lit window, he imagined happy families getting ready for bed and couples cuddled together watching television. These thoughts brought him back to happy memories of his own childhood, followed by his brother's accident and the general uneasiness which had been in the back of his mind ever since. It seemed that having a few drinks and being sociable had only worked as a brief distraction. As always, he returned to this minefield of thoughts and images.

After passing a patch of light from a street lamp, Richard

stumbled over a break in the footpath. Losing his balance, he landed on his knees in the grass beside the road. With his head swirling, he crawled over to a nearby tree. He closed his eyes, hoping the spinning would stop.

Shannon's warm smile came into focus in his mind's eye as he sat in the shadows. Reaching out, he stroked her face, as he had done in the past. When he drew his hand back, it seemed that smudges had appeared on her skin. "No, no, what's going on?" he heard himself cry. He tried to brush them away gently, but each time his hand met with Shay's skin, more marks appeared. "Shay, please tell me what's happening, I don't understand." Throughout this time Shannon's face still had a gentle caring smile, despite the dark smudges that bloomed across her face. As he drew back, he realized that the smudges were bruises.

"Oh no, no! Shay, I'm so sorry. I can't believe I did this to you. I never meant to hurt you."

As he spoke he backed away in horror, wanting to put space between himself and Shay, so he couldn't inflict more damage.

Some hours later, Rich felt himself falling, and he woke to find his face pressed to the damp grass and the solid tree still at his back. As he lay on the grass, he felt wetness on his cheeks, tracks of tears making their way across his skin as he sobbed with the remembered guilt and horror from his dream. "I need to make this right with Shay. I can't keep hurting her," he told himself, slowly pushing himself up from the cold damp ground.

Looking around groggily, he tried to get his bearings, flinching at the cold wind.

After finding his way home and warming up with a hot shower, Richard's mind was clearer. It was almost possible to brush aside the images from the dream. But at the same time he knew that seeing Shannon and finally trying to explain things to her was the only way to make things right for them both.

As he headed to the kitchen, Richard tried to figure out how to approach Shannon and get a chance to talk with her. They had barely talked in the past few weeks since their break up; it had seemed an unspoken agreement to give each other space. He wasn't sure how to find an opportunity for them to talk together.

Chapter Twenty

A couple of days later, during his free class before lunch, Richard went down to the local bakery to get some hot chips. Usually there was a ready supply in the warming cabinet, but the shop assistant told him that the fresh batch would be ten minutes away. Since he had time to spare, Rich took a seat at the one table in the shop. It was next to the window, where he could watch people passing. It was at this point that he noticed a familiar face. Shannon's mum was about to enter the bakery. His stomach lurched. Just as he had been avoiding Shay, he had also avoided her mum. He didn't know what Shannon had said to her mum about their breakup, and how Mrs Carlisle would react to him.

As Shannon's mum entered the shop, Richard gave a brief smile of acknowledgement when their eyes met. He didn't want to actually be rude, but he also hoped she wouldn't decide to come over and talk to him. Even though he had made the decision to talk to Shannon, there was a whole lot of difference between that scenario, and having to deal with a protective and angry mum. He was all too familiar with that, after seeing his own mum facing off with doctors, therapists and officials for years on his brother's behalf. So when

Shannon's mum turned from the counter and came towards him, he felt his stomach drop in dread. She approached with a neutral expression on her face that didn't give him any clues.

"Hi Richard," Evelyn greeted him calmly. "How come you're not at school today?" she asked, in a concerned tone.

"Oh, I am." Richard indicated his bag under his seat. "It's a free class and I had a major craving for some potato wedges. Thought I'd get down here before the main lunchtime rush..."

Evelyn nodded. "Sounds like a good idea. I certainly enjoy a hot lunch on days like this," she gestured out at the heavy grey skies.

When there was no further comment from Evelyn, Rich decided to fill the silence.

"So, umm, how are things going with you and Shay? It's been a while since we've spoken, since, you know, Shay and I broke up," he finished awkwardly.

"Really? I'm surprised by that. From what Shay said, I got the impression that you guys ended on good terms?" Evelyn said sounding puzzled.

"But in answer to your question, we're doing okay. Shay went through a rough patch. You might have noticed she was away from school for a bit, but she's coming back to being more herself. She's had a lot of support from Katey and some of her other friends. But we can all do with some extra support, right?" she said, giving Richard a direct look. "Perhaps you should reconnect with her... I mean, I don't want to assume anything, but you have both known each other and been friends for so long, that it seems sad that you should lose contact."

Rich cleared his throat. "Yeah, actually I was just thinking the same thing. But I didn't want to push her into something if she didn't want to see me."

"If you don't want to approach her at school, why don't you just text her?" Evelyn said.

After returning to school with his parcel of potato wedges, Richard wandered around the grounds. He found himself keeping a look out for Shannon. He felt it was time to commit to having this conversation, especially after some of the comments Mrs Carlisle had made.

Rounding the corner of the art building, Richard entered the courtyard, which was a sheltered hangout spot for the seniors, with a protective awning and picnic tables. There were several groups of people from his year already there, including Shannon and some of her friends, who were gathered in a corner, sitting around one of the picnic tables.

Approaching the group of girls, he greeted them. "Hey, do any of you want some of these wedges? They're fresh from the Bakehouse and still hot. I think they confused my order, because there's way more here than I planned on eating." He finished with a grin.

The offer was met with smiles and raised hands. It seemed like everyone appreciated hot chips on a winter's day.

As he chatted with the group, Richard saw that Shannon was acting much more like her old self. The familiar spark was back in her eyes and she genuinely seemed happy, enough to share laughs with her friends. There were new things he noticed about her, sometimes she became quiet, but it didn't seem like she was sad or withdrawing, more like she was taking time to observe and listen.

When the bell rang at the end of lunch, most of the group collected their bags and headed off, but a few, including Shay, were slower gathering their things and continued talking. Rich decided that now was as good an opportunity as any to approach Shannon.

"Shay, can I talk with you a second? ..."

The other girls moved on ahead, clearly picking up that this was a private conversation, but staying in calling distance.

"I ran into your mum at the Bakehouse and it made me think about how much I miss hanging out with you."

He reached over and picked up the remaining paper wrapping from lunch, not quite able to make eye contact with Shannon.

"I feel like I messed up in a major way and I owe you some answers. Could we meet up and have a talk?" he asked, apprehensively.

As he waited for Shay to reply, Rich scrunched the bundle of newspaper tightly in his hands.

"Well... can you give me till tomorrow to decide?" Shannon responded. "I've missed spending time with you as well, but I don't want to make life more complicated for myself. I'm just starting to get to a good place with how I'm feeling..."

As Shannon spoke these words, Richard dropped his gaze to the ground, trying to hide his disappointment. "It's okay. I totally understand" he replied in a quiet voice. "Forget I mentioned it." He started to turn away.

"Hold on!" Shannon spoke sharply. "I'm not going to say no right away," she continued in a calmer voice. "This is kind of a big thing to decide. I just need some time to think, so can you just give me that?"

At these words Richard looked up and met Shannon's eyes, feeling more assured.

"Sure, I get that. Thanks for giving me a chance... Just send me a text when you decide." He took a couple of steps backward across the courtyard and tossed the bundle of paper into the bin. "I have to get to class. See you later, Shay." He turned and started jogging away. "Thanks again," he called over his shoulder.

Chapter Twenty-one

Shannon took a big slurp of her soup and decided to launch straight in. "So... Mum, did you run into Richard today?"

"Yes," Evelyn answered. "Why's that?" she responded.

Shannon relaxed a little, having Rich's comment confirmed. "Oh, he was hanging around with our group at lunch today. He was sharing round hot chips. Spending time with him was a bit weird, seeing as he's been avoiding me for a while..."

She stopped to take a bite of buttered toast, her brow creased with confusion.

"After we broke up, we stopped seeing each other outside of class. It was like he just disappeared. I guess I've also been away as well... It really did hurt for a while, but I guess with everything else to think about, missing him wasn't such a big thing as it could have been ..."

"That's understandable, you've had a lot to deal with recently." Evelyn reached over and squeezed Shay's hand. "How are you feeling, after spending time with him?"

Shannon blew on her mug of soup before taking another mouthful, stalling for time to make sense of her thoughts.

"Umm, ..." she sighed after swallowing her soup. "I was a

bit weirded out, like I said, and I guess I'm a bit angry that he would suddenly just appear again, after not being around and probably avoiding me. But he says he wants to explain, and he wants a chance to make things right with me, and he was being all sincere and sweet like he used to be, and I just don't know... It's really hard to decide. I mean, I think a part of me still misses the relationship we had, but there are other parts of my brain saying, why give him a chance, and why waste energy on something that's over?"

"That is a lot to make sense of," Evelyn nodded. "Do you have any idea what it is that he wants to explain to you?"

"Not really... I mean, I can't really think what he could have to explain... Maybe he just wants to clear his conscience?" Shannon continued to eat in silence for some time, with an expression of deep concentration.

"Meet after class at my place on Friday?~Shay"

Shannon looked at her phone, almost wishing she could pull the message back from the ether. There was now no escape from facing Richard and whatever he had to say. The decision had not been made on the spur of the moment. In fact, she had been so hung up on whether to say yes or no that she had called her counsellor, to talk it through.

Chapter Twenty-two

"I'm here~Rich"

"Come in. Back garden~Shay"

Shannon turned when she heard the back door open. Richard was coming down the ramp that ran off the deck. She put on a welcoming smile, trying to appear more at ease than she felt.

"Hey," they both spoke at the same time, and then laughed nervously.

"Thanks for seeing me," Richard said, somewhat stiffly. Pulling his backpack off, he flopped onto the outdoor seat.

After a tense silence he spoke. "I don't really know where to start... but I guess the best place is with my brother."

Shannon looked puzzled.

"When I was growing up, my brother was my hero..."

"I don't remember you ever talking much about him. How does he come into this situation?" Shannon interrupted.

"Just give me a minute," Rich replied. "Anyway," he cleared his throat and continued. "He's four years older than me, and was always doing all these cool things with his friends, like motocross and skateboarding and all this other stuff. But then he had an accident. It was totally out of the blue... It nearly wrecked our family. But he did survive, just. Since the accident he's been a quadriplegic and in an electric wheelchair."

Digging into his bag, he pulled out his phone and flicked through until he found what he wanted.

"Look, here's a picture."

Shannon reached over and took the phone. On the screen were two guys, Richard and another guy who looked very much like him, he had the same hair and eyes. They were sprawled out on a big bed with the sun streaming in over them. Both guys had matching smiles and were wearing the same rugby team's colours. Looking closer, Shannon could see the corner of a big flat screen TV at the end of the bed, showing a sports field. They were obviously watching a sports match together.

"That was taken a couple of weekends ago while we were watching the match."

Handing the phone back, Shannon asked, "Why did you never mention this before?"

"That's the thing... I don't really know. I guess I never really dealt with what happened to Tim. It just got really crazy in my head for a while, because I could see what you were dealing with, but I couldn't get through my own issues to be there for you. I felt pretty useless and I guess I just freaked out... again." He reached up and tugged his fingers through his hair, obviously tense.

Shannon nodded in encouragement. Things were starting to make sense at last. But Rich's last word — "again" — stuck out for her.

"What do you mean, freaked out again?"

"Well, do you remember what I was like when we first met?" he responded.

"Yeah, I met you at the school orientation day. There were all the introductions and activities, with everyone getting ready for the year. You hardly said five words in that first day that I can remember. It made me think you were new to the school as well. That was one of the reasons I first wanted to get to know you, being new students together and everything. While I was settling in, other people told me that you had a reputation for causing trouble and that I should be careful, but I already knew what it was like to be judged and have people hold things against you. I wanted to get to know you more and decide for myself."

"Yeah? True? I spent so long being angry and rejecting people that they all gave up. That's why they were warning you, they had good reason not to like me after I'd been getting in fights. I guess I got suspicious of people and they got suspicious of me. That's why it took me so long to let my guard down and ask you out." Richard smiled shyly.

The quiet that had fallen between them felt more comfortable, as they soaked up the pleasant warmth of the spring sunshine. It was one of the first days when it had been possible to sit outside without wearing winter layers.

The peace was interrupted by a giggle from Shannon.

"Remember our first date?" she asked. "You came to my place and we tried making Bolognese pasta... I managed to spill the bottle of sauce down me and the pasta all ended up sticking together in the pot because we got distracted play-fighting with the spilled sauce..." Shannon laughed. "After that I got banned from cooking for a while... I think there are still a few stains on the ceiling."

"Oh man. Yeah, I remember." He laughed too. "Mum had such a tantrum when I got home covered in tomato stains. She made me spend the whole weekend trying to get the marks out. But I didn't care, figured it was worth it after having such a good time."

This memory helped ease both Shannon and Richard into more of a sense of comfort with each other as they remembered the fun they'd had together in the past. When the conversation paused, Shannon's face turned more serious.

"Tell me more about your brother? I'm really curious now to know what he's like... If you don't mind."

"I don't really know how to describe him... I mean, he's my big brother... He loves sports and nature and music... he always has music playing. I guess he's a pretty smart guy as well. I found out the other day that he's teaching himself to code."

Shannon looked blank.

"You know, computer coding, like writing programs and stuff," Rich clarified.

"Oh right," Shannon nodded.

"Yeah, I always thought Tim was just watching videos or something online just for fun, but we were talking the other day, and he started showing me all this complicated but cool stuff that he'd been looking at online. I mean, he even has this whole online community that he's part of..."

"I don't mean to sound dumb, but how does your brother use the computer, if he can't use his hands?"

"He's got a few adapted things, like this program that means he can type using a keyboard on the computer screen, and he has this pointer stick that he controls with his head, that directs the mouse on the screen as well. It's all pretty cool... He got set up with the tech stuff a couple of years ago, but I never really asked what he was using it for 'til now."

"That sounds awesome. I never would have thought about things that could make a computer more accessible." Shannon smiled. "But I guess there are all kinds of things out there to make doing things easier... If only there was something that made decision making easier..."

"Yeah, the teachers keep yapping about applications for university and apprenticeships and all that stuff. I'm really over it. It's bad enough dealing with practice exams and finals," Richard said. "Umm, do you mind if I go get a drink? I'll get you one if you like."

"Sure, thanks. You remember where the glasses are?"

"Yeah, no problem. Be back in a minute." Richard said, getting up from the padded outdoor chair.

As he headed into the kitchen, Rich thought back on conversations he had overheard at school. Pretty much everyone had some kind of idea about what to do once they finished school. Some talked about getting into university, others were going into trades, but a few had been really uncertain, and just seemed like they either didn't care or were overwhelmed by the situation. Thinking about all of the choices was pretty stressful, but his conversation with Tim had actually helped him figure things out.

After filling two glasses, he was about to step back from the bench when he saw a pack of biscuits on the bench. Tucking them under his arm, he stepped back toward the door, noticing that the door handle was new. It was a bar handle which he could open without having a free hand. Setting everything down, Rich said in a satisfied tone, "Pretty impressed with myself, didn't even drop the biscuits. I hope you didn't mind me grabbing them, they were sitting on the bench. Looked like they were waiting to be eaten."

Shannon didn't react to what Rich said, other than to nod and make a sound of agreement. But as Rich was opening the packet, she brought her attention back to the present and spoke again.

"What scares me most now is the prospect of leaving everything I'm used to and the people I trust. It's so much more daunting having to cope with the complications of being in a wheelchair... I'm more used to it now, but it's still something I struggle with on a daily basis. Some days I wake in the mornings and go to roll out of bed like before, but then reality crashes back in on me."

"Wow, that must be tough." Rich spoke sincerely. "It reminds me of something Tim told me... He was describing how sometimes he'll dream that he can still run and do all the other things he used to do, and he'll wake up feeling like he can do the same thing. He said it's like his brain and imagination aren't related to what limits his body has or something. When he told me that, I couldn't imagine how hard that must be, but he explained that it's like, if he wants to do something all he has to do is figure out how to get around his body, because his brain is ready for whatever. It's something that he's figured out to adjust to all the changes, I guess. He told me that he's got a lot better perspective from meeting all these different people online. Some of them are in the same situation as him and are doing all kinds of cool stuff; studying, working, having families. It's like the more he's looked out, the more options he's seen.

I mean, when I came to him and complained about all the pressure on us choosing what to do after school finishes, he said: 'Try things till you find where you fit. Don't stay stuck where you are because of fear.' "

Shannon reached across and took a chocolate biscuit, chewing as she thought about what Richard had said.

"That's a big leap for most people. I mean, it's scary enough to consider being stuck with only a few options, let alone a future where anything is possible." She finished doubtfully. "I bet your brother didn't think that way from the beginning." Her words held a slight challenge.

Richard paused for a minute before answering, looking down at his hands.

"I guess not. But to tell you the truth, I don't really know... Tim got injured about seven years ago, he was only 15, and for years after I just didn't know how to relate to him. It's only been lately that we started getting close again. I feel like I actually have my brother back." He dropped his head into his hands.

"But the ridiculous thing is, I never really lost him in the first place." Richard's words came out with a broken edge.

Shannon watched Richard silently for several minutes, observing him struggling to control his emotions and thoughts. She could see changes as he shifted his posture and noticed the gradual relaxing of his shoulders and straightening of his spine. When he looked up again, after rubbing his hands across his face, she could tell he was more settled. After a while, she felt it was okay to ask the question that had been bubbling in the back of her mind.

"What changed with you and your brother, to bring you together after so long?"

Rich looked at Shannon directly. "In a way, I reckon you had something to do with it... I don't really get why, because after you had your accident, I started feeling all the same things that I went through when Tim got hurt. Everything made me angry, because no one seemed to get that I had lost my big brother, but I was still seeing him every day. It was a pain that just wouldn't go away for so long, because I didn't have any way to make sense of it. But things started changing as I got to know you, and then after your accident I guess some things started to click when I saw you going through everything. In a weird way, seeing you process everything was like watching a movie play out." Shannon frowned at this.

"I mean, I still had feelings for you, and felt bad for what you were dealing with, but I guess I just had more distance to see everything from the outside once we broke up. Seeing your good days and bad, I guess I just found ways to make sense of things with Tim, by seeing you going through it."

Shannon looked at Richard for a moment in awe.

"Wow, that sounds like I was the worst case of ripping the Band-Aid off! I had no idea you had gone through all that stuff with your brother. After not wanting to judge you when we first met, now I'm feeling bad for thinking so badly of you when we broke up."

Richard shifted awkwardly in his seat.

"That's okay, I would have judged me for being such a d-bag. I mean, there are heaps of people who can put aside their issues to be there for the people who are important in their lives. I guess I just wanted to get this stuff out in the open, and hoped that it might be enough for us to be friends again..."

Chapter Twenty-three

Rolling out of the building where the exams had been held, Shannon squinted at the sunny sky. It was such a relief to be out of the chilled and claustrophobic space, where rows and rows of her classmates had spent the last three hours hunched over desks. Shannon sat with her eyes closed, basking in the knowledge that this was the final exam of her high school career. Katey and several others came over.

"I'm so glad that's over," Katey said. "How did it go for you?"

"I'm a bit nervous about that essay question about comparing the narrative devices used in the two Shakespeare pieces..." Shannon confessed. "But other than that, not so bad."

Some of the others nodded. One of the girls turned her face up to the sky with her eyes closed. "I swear I can feel my stress evaporating in this gorgeous sun."

Ashlee sighed, stretching her arms over her head. "I'm not even done with exams yet, but all I can think of is sunbathing and a day at the beach."

"Don't get ahead of yourself, we both have to hang on a bit longer," another grumbled.

"Yeah you're right. Come on then, let's go do some more study and leave these lucky ones to keep gloating." Ashlee grabbed her friend around the shoulder and marched away.

Chapter Twenty-four

"I want to finish by saying how fantastic it has been to work with this council throughout this busy year. You have all done yourselves proud, and you have set a great example for the incoming senior student council," Ms Maclean said, from the head of the meeting table.

"I hope you all have a relaxing summer and some time to prepare for your future plans. Also, one last thing — please feel free to drop in and see us if you are passing through. It's always nice, even for old dinosaurs like me, to see how our past students are doing with their lives," she finished with a smile. "Thank you all and good luck."

As they filed out of the room, many of the student council members stopped to shake her hand or give her a hug.

Shannon was taking her time putting away the notes from the meeting. She was thinking about what the group had accomplished. It was satisfying to think back on the events they had organized and the changes they had been part of putting in place. As she was about to leave, Ms Maclean called her name.

"Shannon, would you mind waiting a minute please? I have a favour to ask...

"I'm sorry that it's so last minute, but I was wondering if you would please make a speech to the senior graduation and prize-giving."

When Shannon didn't immediately respond, Ms Maclean continued: "I had meant to speak to you about this before exams, but things got rather hectic, and I didn't want to bother you right in the middle of your own exams."

Feeling surprised and puzzled, Shannon nodded slowly. "Yes, sure, I guess I can do that. I'm just curious though, why was I chosen out of all the seniors?"

Ms Maclean smiled. "It was actually your fellow council members who nominated you. Usually it is the chairperson of the council who speaks for the group. You were the originally elected chairperson, and they wanted the best representative of leadership, hard work and achievement from the council. As it happens, I am absolutely in agreement with their decision."

Shannon felt slightly overwhelmed at the vote of confidence from her fellow council members and friends.

"Thank you Ms Maclean. I'm sure I can figure something out. I wouldn't want to let them down after that compliment." She smiled widely. "I'll see you at the prize-giving."

Chapter Twenty-five

"Why did I have to agree to do this speech?" Shannon huffed, tossing her pen down on the table in front of her.

"What's that grumbling about?" came Koro's voice over the fence.

"Oh, Koro! Come and help me! I'm supposed to be writing a speech for the senior prize-giving next week. It's only a few days away and all my brainpower has gone since my last exam. I've spent the whole morning staring at my computer screen, trying to figure out something to write. I came out here hoping I'd get some inspiration."

While she was speaking, Koro made his way through the gate. He stopped by the outdoor table.

"Well, I'm not a speech maker myself," he said, taking a seat with a soft grunt. "But how about we forget that for a bit and just relax and enjoy this lovely day?" He waved his hand at the bright blue sky and the dappled sunlight in the garden.

"I always find when I paint that it's better to give ideas their own time and space to come out in the open, rather than struggling to drag them out onto the page. It never worked so well when I tried to force it."

"That sounds like a great idea," Shannon sighed, resting her elbow on the edge of the table and dropping her head onto her palm. "I can't believe I'm still so worn out, exams never used to wipe me out so much."

Koro chuckled. "I wouldn't expect much less, with how hard you've been working. You're clever, but unless you're not telling me something, you aren't Superwoman."

Shannon responded with a half-hearted laugh. He continued: "Did I ever tell you about how I went from being a boat builder and carver to a painter?"

Shannon looked up at him without lifting her head. "No, but I just assumed you took classes after your accident and then got famous...?"

"Oh no, no, ne kotiro. It wasn't anything like that simple. It was actually something of a long road." Koro stared off into the distance as he thought back to his youth.

It was a bright, hot day and he was pulling on his work shirt, when he heard the flat deck truck rumbling outside the gate. The day of labour in the packing shed was about to start. He was still the new guy in the group, but as he climbed up onto the back of the truck he was greeted by faces that were beginning to be familiar. "Morena all," he greeted them, settling in for the ride to the work buildings.

He felt lucky to have got this job up in Pukekohe. His uncle's brother knew one of the men in charge of hiring. After spending more than a year floating about doing odd jobs in his home community near the west coast, he had been encouraged to look for work further afield. So when he had heard about this job sorting fruit, which fortunately he could do with one hand, he had pretty much started work immediately.

One afternoon during a brief smoko break, he had sat down on a pile of old packing cardboard. As he was sitting there sipping his billy tea, he started tracing shapes onto a flat piece of card. He was really focusing on what he was doing. He had an image of his mum in his mind. When he got up at the end of his break, one of his workmates came past and noticed. "Pretty good drawing cuz, who's te ruahine?"

Artie looked back down at his doodling. "You think?" he asked. "It's supposed to be my Mum."

"Yeah, I reckon it's pretty good."

At that point the conveyor belt motor cranked to life and the two guys took up their places on the line.

Koro blinked and swatted away a fly that was hovering around his head. "So that's where I started my art," he said to Shannon. "But it took me a lot of practice, and hard work and a bit of good luck to get noticed by the people who actually helped me build my reputation."

Chapter Twenty-six

Shannon forced herself to keep eating, slowly picking up her toast and taking a small bite. Her nerves had set off a flock of butterflies in her stomach and it wasn't making it easy for her breakfast to settle.

"What are you wearing for the prize-giving, Shay?" her mum asked as she sipped her coffee. "I have to make sure we colour coordinate," she teased.

"We aren't going to a dance together," Shannon replied. "You should wear whatever you like, as long as it's not older than me and it doesn't have spots or animal prints," she smiled.

Feeling in a brighter mood after her mum's joking, Shannon went to get ready.

She changed into her loose silk summer pants and a fitted sky blue halter-neck top to match, and added a cropped blazer to finish. Turning to face the full length mirror that hung beside her dresser, Shannon set to work on her hairstyle and makeup, occasionally reaching into drawers for products.

Chapter Twenty-seven

Shannon looked out at the faces of her friends and classmates in the audience. She had to struggle to keep listening to the principal's words, as the final certificates were presented. Her nerves kept rising up and threatening to take over. Even after spending the better part of the week writing and practicing her speech, Shannon still felt the pressure and anticipation bubbling in her stomach. Most of the awards had been presented; now it was time for the last part of the event.

The crowd clapped after the principal's address, and Shannon was announced as the next speaker. The wait and pressure was nearly over, but her stomach still flipped in reaction.

Shannon started making her way to the centre of the stage. "Alright. I can do this, I can do this," she chanted to herself.

Looking out across the crowd, she took a deep breath. "I would like to start my speech this evening by telling you a story. It isn't something funny or creative, but I hope what I have to say will be encouraging and maybe give my fellow graduates something to think about."

"At the beginning of this year I was a senior representative netball player and I was just like everyone else here... My head was full of plans and I thought I had my future totally set. But then, out of nowhere, things changed dramatically, and here I am sitting in a wheelchair, which I now know will be a part of the rest of my life."

She looked out into the audience and focused on Koro for a moment, uncertain about whether she had the courage to keep speaking.

"Following my accident, I spent a long time recovering in the hospital and then the spinal injury clinic. After a while, being in hospital was comfortable. I felt secure and I got used to the daily routines of checks, visits and therapy. New patients on the ward came and went and I felt like I belonged. But when I came home, even though things were familiar, things also felt scary and traumatic. I was faced with a whole new set of challenges and changes..."

Shannon looked down and flipped to her next prompt card.

"I feel like this new phase in our lives, over the next months, will be like that for all of us. There are lots of changes and options and decisions to be made. These life-changing events happen to all of us. Everyone makes sense of these experiences differently. Whether we realize it or not, graduating high school really is a life changing event. For some of us it is a time of incredible highs and a sense of excitement and anticipation. Others may find it overwhelming and struggle to let go of the familiar and safe environment we are used to. And also people can find themselves experiencing a mix of these feelings."

At this point Shannon paused and cast her eyes over the crowd. She could see she was holding their interest and attention.

"These times of change always present challenges. Leaving the familiar environment that most of us have spent the last five years in can feel like being kicked out of the nest and not having any idea of how to fly..." Shannon felt her voice catch with emotion, and she cleared her throat.

"This new challenge, that is coming to all of our lives, may not be easy, but it is part of the process of us growing into who we will become. This process of leaving the nest, and overcoming the challenges that come with it, takes being able to adapt and face our challenges head on. It isn't something any of us should have to do alone. I, for one, count myself lucky to know that I have a number of people in my life who have my back, as I face this new phase."

As she spoke, Shannon sought out the faces of her mum and Koro. They were sitting together in the second row, amongst the other families in the audience. Koro was wearing his suit, and he looked very handsome and tidy. Her mum was sparkly and polished, in a floral print dress and her hairstyle decorated with a colourful pin stuck through the centre. Both had beaming smiles directed at her. She saw her mum dabbing away happy tears.

"I'm still dealing with all the physical changes, the therapies and specialist's visits. It's still a challenge every day, but I'm determined to work towards getting stronger. I want things to remain as normal as possible, I want people to realise that I'm still the same person, and I need people to treat me the same way as before. When people treat me differently, it's like the old me, the real me becomes smaller and harder to hold onto.

"Having my life changed so drastically seemed like the worst thing imaginable, but it has actually brought my mum and I closer. We have shared a few tearful conversations, both at home and in the counsellor's office, but it has helped us realize how important we are to each other and how strong we are as individuals and as a team. The other upside is that it has helped me to really appreciate the part that other people, like my friends and my Koro, play in being there during my good days and bad. It is because of them that I have started to see there is hope and so much opportunity in my future."

As the final notes of the closing performance faded out, the Dean of the senior class stepped up to the microphone. "On behalf of the faculty and all the families here today, I want to once again congratulate the graduating senior class for their achievements. Will you all please join me now in giving one last round of applause?" At these words, the entire crowd started to clap and cheer.

As Shannon looked around, she saw students reaching out and hugging one another or shaking each other's hands. Families began gathering around their children. There were so many smiles and such a warm feeling in the crowd that Shannon felt tears welling up. Warm arms circled her shoulders.

"We did it," came Katey's excited voice, close to her ear. "We can finally move on to something bigger and brighter," she continued as she sat down next to Shannon.

Before Shannon could respond, Koro and her mum appeared through the crowd with big smiles on their faces. Both adults hugged Shannon. Evelyn hugged Katey, and and Koro shook her hand.

"I'm so nervous about waiting for our exam results... it's been bad enough other years, but now admission to my Tech course is hanging in the balance," Katey said dramatically.

"What are you talking about? I swear you have never got anything below a merit grade," Shannon responded, as Katey was called away to another huddle of friends and family.

"Well done girl. You did so well with your presentation. I wouldn't have known you were nervous if you hadn't mentioned it every ten minutes on the way here." Koro smiled widely and patted her shoulder. "I wouldn't think even the Prime Minister could have done better."

Evelyn nodded in agreement. "I absolutely agree. I would have been a wreck if I had been asked to present to a school assembly when I was your age."

Shannon felt pride swell up at their words. It really had felt so important to try and get her presentation just right. The audience had been so encouraging in their response, and it had felt so good having her mum and Koro and her school friends in the audience as support.

Various other friends and a couple of teachers came over to their little group, to congratulate and farewell Shannon.

"That was a marvellous speech, Shannon. I thought you did such a great job of picking up on points you shared in your class presentation. It really has been quite an extraordinary year for you," Mrs Jones told her.

It was great to be finishing school on such a positive note, Shannon thought. It had been such a struggle when she had first returned after the accident. But now, all the people who counted in her life had found ways to adjust and had come to accept her "new mode of transport" as just an aspect of her life, rather than a strange and awkward elephant in the room.

"I don't know about you, but I feel like a celebratory lunch is in order," Evelyn commented, as she dug around in her purse for the car keys.

Shannon looked around, checking that she'd said goodbye to everyone.

"Sure, that sounds good," she said. "You're coming to lunch as well, aye, Koro?"

"Of course, child. I'd love that. It's not often that this old man and his suit get to go out. Let alone with two lovely ladies such as yourselves. Oh, and remind me I've got a surprise for you at home." He grinned cheekily, before hoisting himself up from the seat.

They had just reached the door when Shannon heard Richard calling her name. A second later, he appeared at her side. "Hey, I'm glad I caught you before you left. I wanted to say congrats on your speech. It was totally unexpected to see you go up and present in front of everyone but it was so awesome. Seriously, I think it hit home for a few people." He looked down and began scuffing the floor with the toe of his shoe awkwardly. "I just…"

"We'll see you at the car, Shay," Evelyn called back, as she and Koro continued out the door.

"Hey, sorry. What were you going to say?"

"Oh. I guess, just good luck with your plans and everything. I hope it goes really well for you. I better not hold you up from getting away." He started to turn away.

"Hold on." Shannon reached out for Richard, grabbing his wrist to stop him from leaving. "We could catch up before Christmas and maybe again round New Year, if you're going to be around…?"

Richard looked uncertain. "Uh. Yeah. That would be cool, if you're not busy or away or whatever… I wasn't sure if you would want to hang out again, after last time."

"I thought we had sorted out that I'm not still angry at you about all the stuff around our break-up." Shannon squeezed his wrist to emphasize her words. "It was the best for both of us. Besides, having good friends to stay in touch with, going into whatever university life throws at us, is the most important thing, don't you think?"

Rich smiled, looking more relaxed at her words.

"Cool. I'll text you soon and we can sort something out." He placed his other hand over Shannon's hand, which was still circling his wrist. He squeezed briefly before letting go.

It was the most contact they had had since the night they had broken up. Rich thought perhaps it should have felt strange, but it didn't. Maybe Shay was right. Maybe it was for the best that they had ended things when they did, rather than letting things become really poisonous between them.

An older woman's voice came from nearby. "Richard! Come on, we need to get going..."

Rich looked over his shoulder and waved. "Um, I better go. Nan is getting antsy about getting home in time to help with lunch... Can I... give you a hug? You know, for Christmas good wishes and everything...?"

Shannon's face lit up in a bright smile. "Totally," she responded, holding her arms out.

They embraced comfortably for a minute, before going off to their own family lunches and celebrations.

Epilogue

Shannon was melting in the heat of the mid-summer day. The fan was on full, while she worked on a seating plan for the sports conference that was being held at the renovated clubrooms. She had been surprised to be offered a job by the conference organisers three weeks into her summer break, but she was pleased to have a distraction from worrying about her university applications.

While she was trying to figure out the last few tables, Evelyn came in from the garden. "Got the mail," she said, sifting through the envelopes. "Not much interesting... oh, except for this one." She waved an envelope at Shannon. It had an official crest, which meant it was from a university.

Shannon felt her stomach drop. Nervously, she reached for the envelope. Before she opened it, she glanced over at the surprise present Koro had given her after graduation, hanging on the wall. It was the beautiful painting she'd admired in his workroom, the young woman surrounded by the shadows of others. She could see the name plaque below the picture: "Never Alone." This reminder that she wouldn't have to face her future by herself gave her the resolve to open the envelope.

"Guess what I'm going to be doing next year...............Studying in Auckland ? I got accepted."

As soon as Shannon put her phone down it started vibrating its way across the table, as her friends responded. She smiled as she flicked through the responses that were full of love and encouragement. It was so different from what she had thought this summer would be like, both before and after her accident. Things weren't going to be the way she had imagined. But she could see that life offered plenty of opportunities, if you just looked out with enough hope.

Acknowledgement of pledgers

Thanks to the pledgers below who generously helped with the publication of this novel. In addition, there were several pledgers who chose to remain anonymous. My thanks go to them, too.

Brent Walker
Linda Lim
Gerry & Greg Glover
Paula Hayes
Mike Alton
Karen Alvarez Perez
Mark Feaver
Glenice McLeod
Rose Morris
Gaby
Chrissy Dryland
Seth
Kat Smythe
Carmel McDermid
Linda Mowbray
Susan Reeves
Raymond Mok

Heather Major
Hollie Doar
Kieran Williams
Eleanor
Andrea Woolsey
Sue & Alan Morris
Robyn Ruddell
Jodi Mitchell
Marin Peplinski
Trudy Hart
Jenna Teesdale
Mark Dobson
Adam Millen
Ian Millen
Barbara & Mike Peplinski
Marcia Millen
Anna Mowbray
Ann & Syd Morrow

About the author

Tegan Morris is somebody who loves a challenge. She likes the excitement and process of overcoming obstacles, particularly when it's not something that seems immediately possible.

She was born with a rare form of muscular dystrophy that means she faces huge physical challenges.

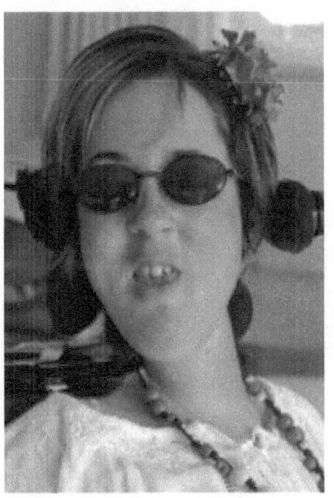

Tegan is a writer, public speaker, advocate, and educator on issues relating to courage, inclusion, and positivity, particularly for those within the disability community. She lives in Hamilton, New Zealand. Tegan publishes weekly online videos focusing on positivity and looking at the lighter side of life.

Tegan on Facebook: https://www.facebook.com/ teganmeetsworld22/

www.ingramcontent.com/pod-product-compliance
Lightning Source LLC
Chambersburg PA
CBHW030654110726
47901CB00002B/708